Seth was so different from Kayla, but he attracted her in a way no other man could.

Seth touched her lips to still the rising objection. Mouth losing its upward curve, eyes searching hers, he said quietly, "You don't have to pretend with me, you know. If you want to have a good cry, I've got just the shoulder."

He'd lost his bantering tone. His face was so tender, her pulse quickened. She swept her hair back and lifted her chin, saying, "I'll keep my tears. He isn't worth it."

Seth's eyes darkened. He captured her chin, his intentions clear enough to send her heart reeling. Yet he hesitated, watching her face. "You're sure?"

"About Richard?" She nodded, melting at his touch.

"That's good." The pressure of his thumb slackened. A finger caressed the delicate line of her jaw. Leisurely. Savoring. Spreading gooseflesh.

His gaze entangled with hers, measuring what lay between them. She saw her own yearnings mirrored in the blue of his eyes. Felt that tingling, tantalizing tug, simple and ageless as time.

"It feels good to touch you," his voice rumbled like distant thunder.

Her skin sizzled, lightning-stricken. "I don't think...."

"Then don't," he stopped her, thick-voiced. "Just this once, don't think."

Terrible advice. She lifted a hand, then let it fall. He took it for acquiescence and framed her face between his hands, rubbing out a raindrop with the stroke of a thumb. Achingly tender. His fingers spread a shower of sparks, trailing through her hair and down her shoulders until the distance shrank and he gathered her in, saying softly, "Come here, you."

SUSAN KIRBY is a freelance writer from McLean, Illinois where she lives with her husband and two sons. Her diversified interests are exhibited in her publishing credits, which include 170 short stories and two novels for children, as well as eighteen romance novels for young adults and adults. *Picture Perfect* marks Susan's *Heartsong Presents* debut.

Picture Perfect

Susan Kirby

Heartsong Presents

ISBN 1-55748-449-X

PICTURE PERFECT

PRINTED IN THE U.S.A.

one

Saturday morning was always a busy time at the post office. Kayla Colter rolled out of bed and hit the floor running. True to form, everything that *could* happen to delay her, happened. It was almost lunch time when she burst into her sister's kitchen. She wiped her feet and flung her coat to one side.

"It never fails! I had key in hand, ready to lock up, when here came Mary Ann with a bulk mailing from the church!"

"I wondered what was keeping you." Shelly scuffed to the stove and turned off the teapot. She arched a knowing smile. "The baby's in the nursery. Tea's almost ready. Go on in."

Kayla paused first to scoop tow-headed Brent into her arms. She gave him a big kiss. "How's my favorite nephew?"

He giggled and wiped his cheek. "Pretty good. I got new boots. Wanna see?"

"I sure do!"

Four-year-old Brent squirmed free and trotted out onto the sun porch. He returned a moment later, a pair of black overshoes in hand.

"Wow! Those are pretty neat. Buckles and everything!"

Brent's fair hair spilled into his blue eyes as he nodded. "I can get in the snow and my feet won't get a bit cold."

"That's great! Are you going to come with me to see your little sister? Or did you want to put your boots away first?"

"I'll put them away," Brent decided.

Kayla continued on to the nursery alone. Her newborn niece lay sleeping in the cradle Joshua had built for Brent four years ago. Shelly'd replaced the bumper pads, sheets, and blanket with a rose-bud print. A dark head, petal-soft cheek, and tiny clenched fist peeked out from amidst all that tufted cotton. Kayla's auburn hair fell forward to curtain her face as she stooped for a closer look. Her heart melted. "Look at you! All pink and soft and perfect."

Shelly scuffed in, two cups of herbal tea in hand. She made no attempt to hide her pride. "So what do you think?"

"She's a keeper, all right. What a beauty!"

Shelly beamed. "Just like her Aunt Kayla."

Kayla considered herself rather plain, but she accepted the compliment with the affection it was given. She stroked the baby's silky head with a gentle finger. "She has Joshua's black hair."

"And twice as much of it."

"Give the man a break." Kayla chuckled and backed away from the cradle as her cup of tea changed hands. She inhaled the fragrance of mint.

Shelly gingerly lowered herself to the daybed. She

waved a hand toward the baby. "Go ahead! Pick her up."

"Are you sure it won't wake her?"

"If she slept through Brent banging on the pots and pans, she can sleep through anything." Shelly swept her hand through her golden hair and smiled.

Kayla settled her cup of tea on the padded changing table. She slung her navy blazer to one side, then carefully slipped her hands beneath the sleeping infant. The baby nestled against her white silk shirt. Her sweet fragility swept over Kayla. Oh what a precious gift! She backed into the white wicker rocking chair, relishing the infant's warmth and the scent of baby lotion.

"Have you picked a name or are you still thinking it over?"

"It's Joy, for certain," said Shelly. "While I was in labor, Joshua read to me from Psalm 30. Those words, 'Weeping may remain for the night, but joy comes in the morning,' pretty much filled the bill! It was just the encouragement I needed."

Kayla smiled her understanding. It had been a difficult pregnancy for Shelly, fraught with complications. This beautiful, healthy child was indeed a joyful answer to prayer.

"Joshua and I think Joy goes nicely with Kayla," Shelly said with a smile. She lifted a finger and wrote in the air as she tried it out: "Kayla Joy. Would that be all right with you? Or are you saving Kayla for a little girl of your own?"

Kayla averted her gaze from her sister's watchful eyes. Would there ever be such a precious gift for her? A wave of longing swept over her. She kissed her niece's silken head. "I'd be honored."

"Good! That's settled," said Shelly with a radiant smile.

The doorbell and Brent's racing steps brought Shelly to her feet. "Brent, honey, don't open the door until Mama gets there!"

Kayla rocked the baby gently, absorbing the tranquility of the nursery she'd helped redecorate. The rosebud wallpaper complimented the deep rose carpet and floral-upholstered daybed. The wicker furnishings were embellished with pastel cushions, eyelet, and lace. Her eyes skipped from the small satin ballet slippers, to a stuffed calico kitten, to the sunbonnet quilt draped over the crib rail—all gifts from Shelly and Joshua's friends. Kayla's own gift had been the picture of Jesus on a flower-strewn hillside, surrounded by children. She'd found the painting at an estate sale and had lovingly restored the antique frame. Someday, she hoped to paint a likeness of the picture. But her art lessons hadn't progressed to the point of including people. She was still perfecting landscapes.

The rocker creaked as Kayla rose and crossed to the window. She raised the ruffled balloon shade to admire her niece in the wintery daylight. Such a perfect creation! The tiny nose, the shell-like ears, the arc of lashes against pearly skin. As the baby snuggled against her, a maternal longing swelled within Kayla until her heart ached. Scarcely aware of the ring of distant voices, she closed her eyes and rode out the intense yearning. Single, twenty-six, her biological clock ticking. Biblical Hannah flitted to mind—how she'd prayed and prayed for a baby and how God had honored that prayer. Hannah, of course, had had a husband.

The click of a shutter jerked Kayla out of her reverie. She turned just as the shutter clicked a second time. The man lowered the camera.

"Hello, Kayla."

Shock rushed along Kayla's nerve-endings at the sight of Seth Brooks, Joshua's brother. His voice vibrated through her as she stood gaping back at him. The face was leaner, etched with lines that had not been there before. Her fingers curled, recalling the texture of his sun-gilded chestnut hair, the gentle strength in those long, blunt-tipped fingers, the tender warmth of his lips. Leave it to Seth to make time fall away with a single hello! Kayla's cheeks flamed. She lifted her guard against a wave of memories as he recapped the lens on his camera.

His eyes twinkled like sunlight on ocean blue. Clad in stone-washed jeans and a cream cable-knit sweater, he strode toward her on the easy long-legged amble that lent itself so well to his height and his leanness. "I'm sorry, I should have asked before I snapped you."

Kayla reined in the bittersweet memories and

found she could smile. "That's what I get for wool gathering. No one told me you were coming."

"Josh called and told me about the baby. I don't think he expected me quite this soon." Tiny lines crinkled about his eyes. With a sweep of long lashes, he smiled and asked, "What's it been—seven years?"

"Shelly and Joshua's wedding," said Kayla, with a steady gaze.

"That's right. You wouldn't dance with me," he teased with the light touch he'd perfected years ago.

"Two left feet," Kayla made an excuse, then blushed at the gentle mockery in his smile.

His blue gaze swept from her face, to the child in her arms, to her navy skirt and dark tights which defined the slim shapeliness of her legs

"You're looking good. I used to worry you were too thin to withstand a good bout of the sniffles."

Hard to believe that this man who'd gained such notoriety with a best-selling travel book was the same man who'd once plied her with vitamin C. Kayla's gaze shifted to the roses he'd tossed to one side. Though it was apparent by the wrappings they'd come from Upton's Floral Shop, she quipped with a flick of her hand, "Still combing the cemeteries, I see."

"They can't all come FTD."

He laughed, and she ducked her head, recognizing the old pattern. From the very first, she'd felt too ordinary for him. Like a marshmallow basking in the warmth of his fire, she'd armed herself with flippancy. It hadn't saved her, though. Inside, she'd been just as soft, just as vulnerable, and saddened by the realization she was too insecure to be comfortable with who she was. Or maybe that had come later when the faith her parents had passed down to her had become her personal faith.

So thinking, Kayla busied herself adjusting the baby's blanket. If only she could regard Seth as simply one more of God's children! But the memories were too rich, too poignant, too painful. Though she'd dated several men since, Seth was the one and only love of her life. Nothing could change the past they'd shared. As the silence grew awkward, she shot a hopeful glance past him.

"Shelly's getting a vase," Seth interpreted her glance. His eyes, as most of her memories of him, were hauntingly blue. They rested on her a moment, assessing her fair cheeks, her gently arched brows, her firm chin, and rich cascade of auburn hair. By the time his gaze shifted to the babe in her arms, she was uncomfortably warm.

"So this is the new addition. Have they named her yet?"

"Yes, they have. Kayla Joy."

"Nice choice." The crevices slashing his sun-browned cheeks deepened when he smiled. He lay his camera on the dresser next to the flowers and reached for the baby. "May I?"

Gently, Kayla put the baby in his arms. She was acutely aware of his closeness as they made the exchange. It was as if his presence filled the whole room, restricting even the flow of air to her lungs. She drew a shallow breath and backed quickly away.

"Tiny, isn't she?"

"Six pounds, nine ounces." Leaving the rocker for him, Kayla took the only other chair in the room.

Seth studied the baby a long moment, then smiled wistfully. "Yessir, this is one neat little gal. Makes you kind of envy Josh and Shelly, doesn't it?"

Surprised, Kayla said. "I thought it was just me."

"Guess it's human nature to want what the other guy's got. Plus what you've got, too," he added with a grin.

Reminded of his work, Kayla said, "Congratulations on the success of *Foot-Loose*. The best-seller's list, no less. I'm happy for you."

"Thanks, Kayla. You always were generous." He smiled as he put the rocking chair into motion.

"I hear you're working on another book," Kayla tried to hide her nerves beneath a flow of conversation.

"Between other projects."

"Busy, I take it?"

Seth sighed. "More so than I'd like to be, at times. I knew if I didn't dash right up to see the new baby, that before I knew it, months would slip by."

"Shelly and Josh are pretty proud. Brent, too, though he's pretending not to be all that impressed," Kayla added.

Seth confided, "I'm not sure he's pretending. He

asked me if I wouldn't rather see his new boots."

Kayla laughed, then whispered, "Just between the two of us, he's got a touch of the sibling rivalry thing. We're doing what we can to diffuse it."

Seth chuckled, then turned his attention back to the baby. He cooed and talked gibberish with such ease, Kayla averted her gaze. Tenderness toward him was a malignancy that had cost her dearly in the past. She crossed to the dresser and hid her face in the bouquet. The heady scent of roses triggered another wave of memories, and unwittingly, she followed it back.

The first flowers Seth had brought her had been yellow roses. She'd worried over the expense, for he'd been working his way through college, tending grounds at a cemetery just a few miles from the University of Wisconsin. The flowers kept coming until she finally begged him not to be so extravagant, only to have him confess that flowers left in the cemetery more than a day or two were disposed of for ease in mowing.

"Seems such a shame for them to go unappreciated," he'd said, ignoring the unwritten law that doomed a flower once it found its way into a funeral spray. Kayla suspected he enjoyed being unconventional, unbound by a reverence for appearances or tradition. He had his gray moods, too, but he wasn't a rebel. He lacked the dark passions. When he penned a column for the school paper, touching upon one or another of society's idiocies, he did it in a capricious way, which made him a favorite on campus, a standout even then.

Brent came bounding into the room, boots in hand. He skipped past Kayla and tossed the boots down at his uncle's feet.

"See? They got buckles, just like Dad's." Brent's white-gold hair fell into his eyes as he fingered the buckles running down the front of his boots. "I can get in snow clear up to my knees. Mama said last week she'd take me, but now she's got to stay home with *her*." He pointed an accusing finger at the baby.

Seth stretched a hand out to his nephew. "Where is it you're wanting to go?"

"To the Maple Camp. They got horses there and everything."

At Seth's questioning glance, Kayla explained, "There's a Maple Syrup Festival going on out at Johnson's Sugar Bush this weekend."

"Sounds interesting."

"It's the most excitement we've had around here since the discovery of that 400-year-old Indian burial site last summer."

Seth returned her smile. "Josh sent me newspaper clippings. I seem to recall artifacts from the dig turned up missing. Did they ever get to the bottom of that?"

Kayla wagged her head. "Josh said there wasn't much to go on."

"So are we going to the Maple Festival or not?" Brent interrupted.

Seth ruffled his nephew's hair. "Maybe your Dad

and I can take you out. Where is Josh, anyway?"

"Dad's already out there. But I couldn't go, 'cause he had to work."

"The sheriff's department sent some men out to keep the traffic moving. They had a mess out there last year," Kayla explained.

Seth smiled at Brent. "What say let's go have a look? I'll snap a few pictures. Maybe we'll run into your dad. I hate to leave without seeing him."

"Uncle Seth, you just got here!" Brent protested.

"I know, buddy. But I can't stay long, or the ole wolf'll be at the door."

Brent's blue eyes widened. "The big *bad* wolf?"

Seth laughed. He explained the expression, then added, "Let's go ask your mom. If it's okay with her, I'll drive you out to the Maple Festival."

"Oh, boy!"

Seth smiled as Brent dashed off. He returned the baby to Kayla's waiting arms, his casual touch sending a wave of heat through her.

"You've let your hair grow," he said, his gaze entangling with hers.

Kayla swept a rich strand back from her face. "It's been long for years."

"It becomes you."

"Thanks," Kayla tried to match his nonchalance.

"You're welcome," he said in that old, familiar, bantering tone.

When he'd gone, Kayla drew a ragged breath only to find a hint of his aftershave lingered in the room.

It was the same fragrance he'd worn years earlier, a musky scent full of associations, all leading back to him.

Kayla's tea went untouched as her thoughts reeled back to her freshman year at college. Seth Brooks had been twenty-six, a journalism major returning to school on the G.I. bill after three years in the service and a couple additional years of gypsy-like travel that had broadened his horizons enough to make him restless. Or maybe the restlessness had come first.

They'd shared a photography class. Creative, artistic, and impetuous, Seth possessed the soul of a romantic and had for a time nurtured two passions—photography and Kayla.

It took him eight days to steal her heart, and though she hadn't seen it at the time, she'd nearly lost her own identity, so taken was she with him. She'd neglected other friendships, quit a part-time job she'd liked with a salary she needed, even cut an occasional class just to spend time with him. He hadn't asked it of her or expected it. But love had had such a hold on her that she lost all sense of balance.

Eighteen months into the relationship, he talked her into marrying him. The only reason she'd held out that long was his confessed agnosticism. Even in her infant faith, she'd seen that difference as a hurdle. Her heart had overruled her better judgment. They'd planned a small wedding, inviting just family members to witness their exchange of vows.

But shortly before their big day, Seth had landed a

freelance assignment with a small but nationally known travel magazine. Kayla had shared in his excitement. It was a tight deadline, and if he were to meet it, he needed to drive to Myrtle Beach right away. Could they go before a justice of the peace, then make the trip together, he'd asked?

Holding out for the planned wedding in her home church, Kayla suggested he go alone, complete his assignment, and return in time for the wedding. Once down there, he discovered a movie being filmed on location, which created all sorts of interesting freelance possibilities. He called, urging her to join him. When she declined, he asked for a few more days, a week at the most.

A week stretched to three, and by the time he returned, Kayla had come to her senses: Seth Brooks wasn't good marriage material. He was a born rover, having chosen a career that legitimized his rambling. She, on the other hand, had roots in Kitterly, Wisconsin, a quiet little town midway between Milwaukee and Door County. An organized, punctual person by nature, she decided after much agonizing deliberation that she could not adapt her lifestyle to that of a man who couldn't keep his own wedding date!

And so they had gone their separate ways. Shelly, by that time, had been dating Seth's brother Joshua—Kayla had introduced them. Their relationship culminated in marriage. Today, Joshua worked for the Kitterly County Sheriff's Department. Shelly wrote verse for a greeting-card company. They shared two beautiful children, the mortgage on a split-level home, and one of the most vibrant marriages Kayla had ever witnessed.

But Kayla's life hadn't been so rosy after the break-up. Caught with a gaping hole in her life, she'd drifted aimlessly from one dead-end job to another. Joshua had been so troubled by her lack of purpose that he'd talked her into attending the police academy. The rigors of the academy taught her discipline of mind and body. Yet a few months as a rookie cop opened her eyes to the deceitfulness and depravation of humanity.

As Kayla arrested suspects involved in everything from petty theft, to domestic violence, to drug trafficking, she ceased feeling sorry for herself, focusing instead on the pain and despair in others. God became real to her as never before. Some of the very people she'd arrested, she visited during her off-duty hours, urging them to give God His place in their lives. Her witnessing hadn't gone over well with the department. Fearing she lacked the necessary mental toughness, they relieved her of her duties.

But God opened doors, filling the voids in her life. She landed a job at the post office, which she liked very much. She was instrumental in starting a prison ministry through her church. She loved being an aunt. She'd started taking art lessons, and there was her interest in antiques. She'd recently purchased Kitterly's small abandoned railroad depot with the idea of turning it into a 'weekend only' antique shop. Her life was full, so full that most of the time, she was too busy to entertain unbidden memories.

Most of the time. Her gaze lifted to the threshold, where Seth had reappeared. His hair was clipped shorter than she remembered. A few errant curls scattered across his brow. He smiled and framed her from where he stood between boxed fingers, spouting captions, just like the old days:

"*Namesakes.* You make a striking picture. May I?" He reached for his camera.

Kayla turned her head.

He chuckled and snapped the photo anyway, saying, "See how you are when I ask?"

"I thought you and Brent were going out to the Maple Camp."

"We are. Would you like to come with us?"

"I came to help Shelly. This is her first day home."

Shelly ducked under the arm Seth had braced against the door jamb. "Go on, Kayla. I need a nap, anyway. There's no reason for you to stay."

"Ride in the sleigh with me, Aunt Kayla. Please?" Brent chimed in.

Kayla hesitated. Perhaps she should go. Prove to herself that yesterday was gone, that she and Seth were two very different people from those soulmates of seven years ago. Maybe she could finally set herself free of all those old memories.

two

Johnson's Sugar Bush was a few miles out of town.
It was a popular attraction. Traffic on the county road
was steady, some of it returning from Johnson's,
some just heading out.

"Are you warm enough back there?" Seth glanced
over the seat of the roomy rental car.

Brent grunted in the affirmative and went on
fishing through the box of shells Seth had picked up
for him while in Sanibel Island two weeks earlier.
Seth turned his attention to Kayla. "How's the career
coming along?"

Kayla smiled. "I'm in striking distance of a real
good opportunity. The postmaster is retiring and I'm
throwing my hat in the ring for his job."

"Good for you! Any notable competition?" Seth
slanted her an attentive glance.

"A few. I'm at peace about it, though. If I get it,
great. If not, I'll assume God has other plans for me."

"Playing post office big time, eh? Good pay, good
benefits, and a good retirement plan. Any other
perks?" he teased.

Kayla chuckled. "More vacation days, plus my
Saturdays are free, which would fit in well with a
project of mine."

"What kind of project?" he asked.

"I bought the old railroad depot with the intention of turning it into an antique shop. Joshua had it moved to the south edge of town for me, which puts it right on the highway leading to Door County."

"I came past it on my way in. I had no idea the building was yours," Seth added. "Great location!"

Kayla nodded. "A friend with some experience in antiques helped me pick the spot. The tracks run just behind it, which adds authenticity. I'm hoping to pull in the tourists."

"Kind of an expensive business to get into, isn't it?" Seth asked, turning down the blower on the car heater.

"I'm just beginning to realize *how* expensive. Buying the land, moving the building, fixing the roof, painting—it all adds up." Kayla swept a hand through her hair and explained, "For a while, I'll solicit antiques to sell on consignment. This friend I mentioned suggested that system. He has a basement full of nice old pieces. Until I build up a good trade, it's the only way I can afford to stock the shop."

"Sounds like you've got a good handle on it. Let me know how it comes out," Seth said.

"Thanks. I will."

As a comfortable silence fell between them, Kayla slipped out of her coat. She gazed at the passing scenery. A recent heavy snow had buried fence rows and draped the branches of pine forests. Snowmobile trails criss-crossed open fields like tracks in a railroad yard.

Fascinated with the sea shells, Brent questioned Seth about Sanibel. Kayla listened to Seth's description of the island paradise. At the beginning of his career, Seth had traveled on a shoestring budget to far away places, freelancing for magazines so obscure, few people had heard of them. But all that had changed when his travel book met with such wild success two years ago. His photos and travel articles now attracted an international readership. Yet he seemed unchanged by the attention. Travel, it appeared, was still the love of his life.

Squinting against the bright glare, Seth plunged his hand into the seat pocket, then reached across Kayla to flip open the glove box. "Are my sunglasses in there?"

Kayla found several rolls of film, the rental contract, a road map, and a proof of insurance card. "Not a sign of them."

"Must have lost them at the airport."

Kayla felt him glance in her direction, as if awaiting some comment. When she made none, he slanted her a grin. "So you're going to let that pass, are you?"

"No point in digging up old bones," she murmured, remembering how his habit of misplacing things used to annoy her.

Seth chuckled as she snapped the glove box closed. He pulled down the sun visor.

"This new book of yours—what's it about?" asked Kayla.

"Route 66." At her puzzled glance, he added, "The famed highway."

"Oh!" Kayla smiled, a sudden remembrance coming to mind. "That was the road west, wasn't it? The summer before I started school, Dad bought a camper. We traveled Route 66 all the way to California. What a trip that turned out to be!"

Seth smiled. "A lot of people have memories of 66. The highway's enjoying a rebirth of popularity."

"You mean it still exists? I thought it disappeared years ago."

Seth wagged his head. "It's been superseded by interstate highways, but most of the old road is still there. Some is abandoned, some is used as access roads. There's been such a revival of interest, a Route 66 Study Act has been signed by the president. The National Park Service is looking into ways of saving and commemorating the remaining highway."

"Really?"

Seth nodded and grinned. "Seems the Mother Road just never dies in the hearts of a lot of folks."

"'The Mother Road,'" Kayla echoed. "Steinbeck called it that in *Grapes of Wrath,* didn't he?"

Seth nodded. "It's also been called the Main Street of America. For nearly fifty years, just about everyone who went west traveled Route 66."

Kayla wondered how Seth was going to make a book out of an old road that had been decommissioned nearly two decades ago. When she asked as much, he wagged his head as if her lack of imagination disappointed him.

"The story is more than a 2,200-mile stretch of road," he explained. "It's the family of people linked by 66. The road represented opportunity to a restless nation. Countless folks followed it in search of their own personal dream. The dreams, of course, were as diverse as five decades of travelers."

Thinking again of Steinbeck's depression-era story, Kayla said thoughtfully, "Not all those dreams came true."

"No, of course not. But the pathos evoked by the saddest of memories somehow contributes to the road's appeal." Warming up to his subject, Seth smiled as he added, "And then there's the people who lived along the road, making their living from those who passed by. Gas stations and restaurants and motels and gifts shops, all of them catering to tourists. Just as you're planning to do with your antique shop. Those are the kinds of people I'm interviewing for my book."

Kayla mused, "If anyone can make it work, you can."

He laughed. "Thanks for your vote of confidence."

Kayla colored. "What I meant to say was—"

"What you said," he finished and laughed again. "You're entitled to your reservations. But I'm willing to bet if you'd spend a week on the old route with me, talking to people, hearing their stories, you'd change your mind."

"Think so?"

"It gets to you, the feeling that there's a pulse still beating beneath that crumbling ribbon of concrete," he insisted.

Kayla smiled, reminded of his passion for pet projects. His child-like exuberance hadn't faded in the years gone by. Secretly glad, she asked, "Have you traveled the whole stretch?"

"At one time or another, but never in a single trip. Until now." Seth adjusted the mirror as he explained, "I got a network executive interested in the highway. He's asked me to produce a special feature on it. He's providing a sound man, a camera man, and Jessica Williams."

Kayla's eyes widened. "Jessica Williams is part of the crew?"

Seth grinned and nodded, rewarded by her surprise. "She'll do the on-camera interviewing. We'll share the narrating."

Jessica Williams was a top-notch anchor out of Chicago who had, in the past several years, gained national recognition with her insightful, hard-hitting journalism. She was a household name. Kayla exclaimed, "On the road with Jessica Williams! Seth, that's big time! Congratulations!"

"I'm having a little trouble believing it myself!" Seth grinned and added, "We're leaving from Chicago a week from Monday. Would you like to come along?"

"My vacation starts that day, so don't tempt me!"

Kayla jested.

"We're taking a van for the equipment, plus I'm driving my motor-home. There'll be plenty of room."

Noting Seth had lost his jocular manner, Kayla angled him a seeking glance. "Are you serious?"

"If you're interested." He stopped at a stop sign, then said as they picked up speed again, "I could use some help taking notes and keeping them typed up. I'm afraid I'll be so busy producing the show, I won't be able to keep track of the details I'll need for my book. How much time do you have off?"

"Two weeks."

"Perfect! We're allowing ten days for the trip."

Kayla wagged her head and smiled. "Thanks for the offer, but I won't be going."

"Are you sure? It's a great opportunity to see the country," he pointed out.

"I know. But I've got things to do in the shop. And besides, I'm seeing someone," she added.

"Hey, this is strictly business. You'll be on the payroll," Seth hastened to assure her. "I'll talk to the guy if you'd like me to."

"No, thanks," she murmured.

"Who is he? Anyone I know?" Seth persisted.

"Richard Farrell. He moved here last summer. It was he who suggested the antique shop."

"Good taste in women and smart, too," Seth said with a grin.

Kayla's color deepened. But she was spared comment when Brent slipped out of his seat belt, squealing, "We're here!" His head popped over the seat between them. "I can't wait to see the horses!"

Kayla pointed out the break in the fence ahead. "Pull up into the field, Seth. We'll have to walk the rest of the way."

"Look at all the cars! There's Dad!" Brent waved to a broad-shouldered man in a police uniform.

Intent on directing cars into the lot, Joshua Brooks was motioning them on when Brent rolled down the window and hollered, "Hey, Dad! Where's the horses?"

Surprised recognition flashed across Joshua's face. Directing them off to one side, he beckoned cars on until there was a break, then loped over to shake Seth's hand through the opened car window.

"It's great to see you. I didn't expect you to come so soon," Joshua exclaimed.

"I had an appointment in Chicago this morning. I figured as long as I was so close, I'd come see my new niece."

"And what'd you think?"

"She's a looker, all right. Is it just me, or does she have Kayla's green eyes?"

Joshua beamed. "Shelly thinks she favors her, though if you ask me—"

"Watch it, bub, I'm all ears," Kayla warned.

Joshua looked beyond Seth and blurted, "Kayla! I didn't see you."

His obvious surprise underscored that Kayla had, in the past, gone out of her way to avoid Seth when he'd dropped by Josh and Shelly's for a visit. He was wondering what to make of her sudden reversal. Riding out the moment with a bright smile, Kayla said, "Your son invited me on a sleigh ride."

Joshua beamed. "The fresh snow should make good sleighing. So how've you been, Seth? Hard at work on the book?"

"Trying to be."

A horn honked. Turning to go, Joshua peered into the back seat and warned, "Stick close to Kayla, Brent. There's quite a crowd. Seth, you're coming back to the house later, aren't you?"

Seth began to protest that his time, this trip, was very short, but Joshua waved aside his remonstrations. "You can at least have dinner with us!"

Seth didn't commit himself. He hit the electric window switch and bumped across the field into a parking place. Kayla, who'd stopped by her house to change, zipped her down coat. She wrapped an emerald-green scarf around her neck and pulled on matching mittens and cap in preparation for the quarter-mile walk ahead of them.

Camera slung around his neck, Seth filled the pockets of his black leather jacket with extra rolls of film. He turned up his collar, stuffed the tips of his fingers into his jean pockets, and fell in step beside her. A stiff breeze stirred his close-clipped curls as they strode down a snowy, tree-lined lane.

Kayla shot him a sidelong glance. "Lost your gloves, too, did you?"

He confessed it with a sheepish grin.

"If you want to trust me with your film. . . ."

He handed over the extra rolls. She stashed them in her coat pockets, freeing up his for cold hands.

At the heart of the maple camp was the sugar house. It was a weathered old building with enough age and charm to catch Seth's artistic eye. He popped the lens cap off his camera and shot it from several angles. There was a line at the door, waiting to go inside to see the clear maple sap being cooked into the thick amber syrup. Kayla pointed out to Brent the steam escaping the picturesque cupola atop the sugar house.

"Mm. Smell the sweetness in the air, Brent?"

Brent took a sniff, then chanted questions about the sleigh ride.

Kayla exchanged glances with Seth. "Maybe Brent and I should check out the sleigh ride while you get some pictures inside."

"Don't you want the grand tour?"

"I bottled syrup for Ben Johnson when I was in high school, I'm familiar with the operation."

"Really? How come I didn't know that?"

"I guess it never came up."

"What other secrets are you keeping?"

Returning his smile, Kayla unfurled the green wool scarf from her neck and arranged it around his. "Tug it up around your ears. This isn't Sanibel Island."

Before he could reply, a familiar voice called out a greeting. Kayla turned, subconsciously lifting her guard. Decked out in high-heeled leather boots, snug-fitting black ski-pants, and a short white rabbit-fur coat, Richard's daughter appeared quite mature for a college sophomore. "Are you waiting for the tour, Kayla?" she asked, cutting gold-flecked eyes at Seth.

"No, Brent and I are going for a sleigh ride."

"There's a line there, too."

"Then you've ridden?" The young woman shook her head, prompting Kayla to invite, "You're welcome to come with Brent and me."

Misha Farrell appeared to consider the invitation, all the while, eyeing Seth. Her dangly earrings caught the sunlight as she cocked her head to one side. "I think I'll wait here with your friend and tour the sugar house."

At the none-too-subtle prompt, Kayla made introductions. "Misha, I'd like you to meet Brent's uncle, Seth Brooks. Seth, this is Misha Farrell."

Misha flashed him a smile from beneath thick tawny lashes. "Say, aren't you the fellow who took all the pictures for that Midwest calendar that was such a rave around Christmas? Joshua Brooks' brother? Sure! Dad got one for Christmas. Speaking of Dad, if you're looking for him, Kayla, try that long building over there."

"He's here?" asked Kayla, surprised. "I thought he was out of town on business."

"He flew home this morning," said Misha. "He'd love to go on the ride with you."

Nodding, Kayla started away. She gave Brent's hand a squeeze as they approached a large, modern out-building tucked back into the trees. "Let's peek inside for Richard."

One end of the building contained historical exhibits concerning the history of syrup making. At the other end were booths hosted by some of Kitterly's charitable organizations. Demonstrations of maple concoctions were interspersed throughout the building, while off to one side, a story-teller was weaving a spell over a captive young audience.

Failing to find Richard, Kayla bought hot cider and cookies. She and Brent sipped their drinks as they tramped through the snow to the field where the sleigh rides were being given. The line was moderately long, but it was a pretty setting. The small field was surrounded by trees. A smattering of people strolled amid the maples, peeking into the sap buckets and sticking their fingers beneath the snow-capped lids to catch a droplet of sap from the spiles.

After an hour of shivering and stamping her feet to keep warm, Kayla was relieved to be at the front of the line.

"You folks'll be next," assured the whiskery-faced old gent who was orchestrating the sleigh rides. Cheeks cherry red, he ducked back into the tiny hut erected to spare him unnecessary exposure.

Sleigh bells rang in the clear cold air as the draft horses pranced around the field. The horses' manes rippled in the breeze, their breath creating cotton clouds of vapor in the bright, frigid air. Kayla saw that Seth had arrived. The green scarf whipped in his face as he tried to capture the scene in his lens.

At the same moment, a familiar voice called out her name. Richard Farrell advanced to the front of the line to join her. Snug in a long wool coat, leather gloves, and felt hat, he slid an arm across her shoulder and planted a kiss on her cheek.

"Misha told me I'd find you here. If I'd known you were coming—"

"I didn't expect to see you here, either. How was your trip?" asked Kayla.

"Productive." Richard glanced around. "Are you alone?"

Assuming Misha had given him the full report, Kayla explained, "Joshua's brother, Seth, came with us."

"The photo journalist?"

She nodded and pointed out Seth, saying, "That's him with the camera."

"What's he doing wearing your scarf?" asked Richard.

Surprised by the irritation in his voice, Kayla said evenly, "I gave it to him. He didn't bring a hat."

"No hat. No gloves. That's about what you can expect from those arty types," Richard said.

"Actually, Seth's very down to earth. Come on, I'll introduce you."

Richard bristled like a dog measuring his opponent and replied, "Let him come to us."

three

Seth tucked the ends of Kayla's scarf into his jacket to keep them from fluttering in front of his lens. The scent of her favorite cologne clung to the scarf. The familiarity of it enveloped him in old memories. Could that account for the wrenching of heart as Kayla, being kissed by the fellow in the long wool coat, found her way into his camera lens?

Farrell looked to be ten, fifteen years older than Kayla. Well fit. Impeccably dressed. Of medium height, with a dash of grey at his temples. Arrogant fellow, jumping line like that, and faintly familiar. Seth paused a moment, trying to place him. Failing, he refocused with cool deliberation. "Smile, Brent."

Brent smiled and Seth took the picture. He caught Kayla in the background, her gentleman friend standing just behind her. Recapping his lens, he strode forward and introduced himself. "I'm Seth Brooks, Joshua's brother."

"Richard Farrell." The man gripped Seth's extended hand.

"Richard has an import business in Milwaukee. He and his daughter, Misha, whom you met earlier, moved into a new home south of Kitterly last spring," Kayla explained.

"You own a retail store, then?" asked Seth.

"It's more of a warehouse. Most of our business is mail order," Richard said.

"I see!" Seth bobbed his head and smiled. "It was a common interest in mail that drew you two together!"

"Nothing so dull as that, was it, dear?" Richard dropped a perfunctory kiss on Kayla's smiling mouth. His intimate smile closed Seth out as he added in a low voice, "The trip seemed endless. I missed my little treasure."

Seth's cold hands tightened around his camera. The nagging sense of familiarity fell into place. The airport! He'd seen the fellow at the airport! And he hadn't been alone.

"Seth had an appointment in Milwaukee, so he came by to see the new baby," Kayla was saying. She tipped her head to look into Farrell's face. "She's so sweet, Richard! Perhaps you can stop by and see her later."

"I don't know. I've got a pretty full schedule," Richard said.

Kayla quickly lowered her lashes. But not before Seth glimpsed disappointment in her expressive green eyes. Trying to make up for Farrell's lukewarm response, he said, "They're naming her after Kayla. Kayla Joy. She has Kayla's eyes as well as her name. A beautiful baby!"

Spots of color flashed on Kayla's cheeks. She smiled and said gently, "I think she looks like her big brother."

Brent's head came up. "Really?"

"You bet!" exclaimed Kayla. "She's blessed to have a brother like you, Brent. Why, I just imagine you'll be her hero."

Brent puffed out his chest. "I swung her cradle today and she stopped crying. She's too little to play, though."

Remembering Kayla's earlier words concerning sibling rivalry, Seth winked at Brent. "She'll be tagging along after you before you know it. Of course, you'll want to look after her a bit. You've been around longer and you know what's what. Isn't that right, buddy?"

Brent kicked at a drift of snow. "She can't wear my boots, though. 'Cause they're black, and black is for boys."

"Guess she'll have to get her own boots," Kayla agreed. She exchanged a quiet smile with Seth and patted Brent's shoulder. "But that's okay. There'll be lots of other things you'll want to share."

The horse-drawn sleigh pulled up with jingling bells and the jangle of harness. The red-capped driver pulled on the reins, stopping almost at their feet.

"Our turn. Up you go. Let's not keep the fellow waiting," said Richard as he helped Kayla into the sleigh.

Seth swept Brent up off the ground, singing out, "Make room for Brent! He's coming in for a land-ing!"

Brent giggled and waved as he settled between Kayla and Richard.

As the horses pranced away, Seth attached the long lens and focused. The graceful shape of the sleigh, the horses' broad flanks, the glittering snow, the winter bare trees made a picture-perfect shot. But Seth's inspiration for treating the festival as a travel feature had waned. His gaze followed the sleigh until it was only a dot on the far side of the field.

Who was this Farrell character, anyway? And who was the woman he'd seen with him at the airport? She'd been quite a looker. Farrell had kissed her with a good deal more passion than that peck he'd landed on Kayla's lips! Little treasure, indeed! Who'd the guy think he was kidding?

Kayla, that's who! Realizing he was getting worked up over something that was none of his business, Seth forcefully redirected his attention and took a close-up of a syrup bucket. He focused with care, catching the drip of sap on the end of the spile just before it dropped into the bucket. Great shot! But he took little pleasure in it. Anxiety gnawed at him.

Of all the women he'd dated, Kayla had evoked the deepest emotions. He'd very nearly married her. Would have, in fact, if she hadn't called it off. It was perfectly natural to feel concerned over this fellow, Farrell. Maybe Josh could fill him in on the guy.

So thinking, Seth tramped back to the parking area, where his brother was directing traffic. Josh was too busy for questions and answers. He hollered, "My replacement comes on duty in half an hour. I'll meet you in the exhibit building."

Seth nodded agreement. The chill wind whipped Kayla's scarf in his face. He shivered and quickened his step, angling toward the exhibit building. The coffee, strong and hot, was just to his liking. He sampled some maple candy and purchased a jug of syrup, then killed what remained of his waiting time listening to the story-teller entertain a flock of kids. His toes were just beginning to thaw when Joshua found him.

"Where's Brent and Kayla?"

Seth explained. Perceiving a slight shift in his brother's expression, he added, "It was plain Farrell didn't want me tagging along."

"I'm sure you've got that right." Joshua rubbed hands red with cold and changed the subject, saying, "I could do with a cup of coffee."

Seth made a return visit to the booth selling coffee and maple-flavored donuts. He filled a tray while Joshua found a table. Curbing his curiosity concerning Farrell, he listened as Joshua skipped from talk of his family to his job with the county sheriff's department.

Cup drained, Joshua checked his watch. "Maybe I should go take Brent off their hands."

"What for? Kayla's nuts about Brent. She's wonderful with him," Seth added.

Josh frowned. "I'm afraid Farrell may feel differently, though. And Brent's sensitive."

"Surely Farrell wouldn't snub a little kid!"

"I hope not. But then, how can I be sure? I hardly know the guy."

Surprised, Seth said, "I was under the impression Kayla's been dating him for a while."

Josh nodded. "Yes, since last summer. But with Shelly and me, he's sort of distant."

"What do you mean?" Seth asked, his curiosity over this man Farrell growing.

Josh helped himself to another donut. He chewed slowly, thoughtfully, choosing his words with care. "Most of the fellas Kayla's dated have been from Kitterly. They come to the house, have cookouts with us, play croquet on the lawn, that sort of thing. It's different with Farrell. He hasn't shown any interest in getting to know us. It's kind of awkward for Kayla. You know how family centered she is." Joshua fell silent. He ran a hand through thinning hair and sighed.

Something in Josh's manner made Seth wonder what he wasn't saying. After a brief pause during which Josh contributed nothing more, he asked, "What about Shelly? How's she feel about Farrell?"

"She says that Kayla's a sensible adult with good instincts concerning people. And that if Farrell's her choice, we need to lend our support, not our reservations."

"Then she's serious about the guy?"

"Could be." Joshua crushed his empty paper cup in

his hand. "If you ask me, he's trying real hard to *appear* to be just what she's looking for."

"Which is?"

"A down-home, one-woman, God-fearing man."

"And you think he's something else?" Seth asked, remembering what he'd seen at the airport.

Joshua lowered his voice. "Partly, I'm confused as to why a guy with a business in Milwaukee would want to live in Kitterly. As much as he travels, you'd think he'd want to be as close as he could get to the city."

Seth shrugged. "He could have small-town roots. Or maybe he's tired of the pollution and crime and traffic jams. A lot of folks want out of the city."

Josh propped his forearms on the table and narrowed the distance until his face was just inches from Seth's. "Farrell moved to Kitterly last spring shortly after that ancient Indian burial ground was discovered. They weren't long into the dig when artifacts came up missing."

Seth looked at him in surprise. "You think he had something to do with that?"

"There's no evidence of involvement on his part. Checking him out was purely routine," Joshua said.

"What'd you learn?"

"Zilch, which in itself is uncommon. People are usually pretty easy to track. Bank records, driver's licenses, real estate transactions, tax records, credit cards, that sort of thing. With Farrell, nothing! It was as if he dropped out of nowhere."

Seth thought he was following his brother's train of thought. Just to be certain, he asked, "So it isn't that you think Farrell was involved in the theft. Rather, that he seems to be a man without a past?"

Josh nodded. "And experience has taught me nine times out of ten, a guy like that has something to hide."

Seth thought of the scene at the airport. He asked, "Did you mention this to Kayla?"

"No. I didn't see much point in alarming her when I've got nothing concrete against the guy. Plus Shelly's warned me to go easy."

"Then why are you telling me?" asked Seth.

Joshua flashed a self-deprecating grin. "Venting concern, I guess. Anyway, you were always good at secrets."

Seth grinned in return. Their father, a traveling salesman, had spent very little time at home during their formative years. But their mother made sure they didn't grow up undisciplined. Seth had, by virtue of silence, saved Josh's hide on several occasions.

Over the rim of his cup, Seth saw Kayla strolling through the exhibits. She was hand in hand with both Farrell and Brent. He was about to confide in Josh what he'd witnessed at the airport when Kayla's green gaze crossed his. Her quiet smile stilled his tongue. How would she feel if she was the last one to learn that she wasn't the only woman in Farrell's life?

Brent suddenly spotted them. He came dashing over to tell them about the sleigh ride. At the same time, Kayla parted company with Farrell. She got in line at one of the refreshment concessions. Seth pushed his chair back. He ambled over and fell in line behind her.

"Now you've really done it! Brent's over there pestering his dad for a team of horses and a sleigh to dash around town in," he said.

Kayla smiled in that old familiar way. "It *was* fun! Cold, though. I hope they have cocoa."

"Still don't drink coffee, huh?" he said, memories stirring. "I don't know about you, Kayla. No vices at all!"

She laughed. "When it comes to faults, you always were easy on me."

He hadn't been easy, though. Not really. He'd broken her heart, broken his own heart too. Despite her warmth, her sweetness, it lay between them. *Keep it light. Keep it easy.* Aware his heart was beating fast, he said, "I think I'll hit the road here shortly. Do you and Brent want a ride back to town?"

"Richard'll take us. But what's your hurry, Seth? Shelly and Josh will be expecting you to stay for dinner."

"A new baby is company enough for a lady just out of the hospital. Shelly doesn't need the likes of me underfoot."

Kayla smiled and let it drop, saying, "It was nice seeing you again. Good luck on your Route 66 project. When do you think it'll air?"

"It'll be a month or more after filming."

"Be sure and let us know, Seth. We don't want to miss it."

"You bet!" Unwilling somehow to say his goodbyes and be gone, he smiled and added, "Sure I can't talk you into coming along?"

She swept her hair back and smiled. "As tempting an invitation as that is, I'll have to decline. Spring's just around the corner, and I've got a lot of work to do, getting my shop ready."

"I wish you well. Both with the shop and the promotion to postmaster." They talked a moment longer, then Seth bid her goodbye. He'd already started away when his gaze crossed Farrell's. Something in the man's narrow-eyed demeanor challenged him. He turned back, saying, "Kayla? Old friends really should do a better job of keeping in touch. I'll send you a postcard now and then, what do you say?"

She smiled and nodded. "That'd be nice. Landscapes, especially. I've just started taking art lessons. So far, landscapes are all I do."

"Art lessons, is it?" He wagged his head. "You want to learn something, you just jump right in, don't you!"

"I learned that from you."

Seth threw back his head and laughed. "Good for me!"

She smiled and replied sweetly, "You *were* good

for me. Good for me and good to me. Makes for nice memories, doesn't it?"

Smile fading, he nodded, then leaned over and kissed her cheek. The scent of winter was in her hair and, beneath that, the old familiar scents of soap and perfume and Kayla. His heart slammed against his chest. He felt both hot and cold as, once more, their eyes met.

Calm, composed, she held steady, murmuring, "Take care of yourself, Seth."

He strode back to the table and visited a few minutes longer before bidding both his brother and nephew goodbye. But it was the look in Kayla's eyes Seth was remembering as he climbed into the Crown Vic, slammed the door, and fit the key to the ignition. She wasn't given to casual kisses or embraces. He'd forgotten that, accustomed to functioning in a world where a kiss was as meaningless as a handshake. And even less binding. But she'd been gracious about it. *Gracious,* not breathless or blushing. No palpitating heart to betray deeper emotions.

Seth's heart was beating fast. He felt breathless, just thinking about it! The feel of the wheel beneath his hands, the accelerator under his foot, soothed him with it's familiarity. Yet he couldn't get that look in her eye out of his mind! She'd looked at him with such gentleness and love. Not the kind of love a woman holds for a man. No. It was similar to the look she'd bestowed on the baby back at the house. And on Brent. A tender well-wishing expression. The flame had died, only friendship remained. Why did that shake him so?

In less than twenty minutes, Seth was heading south on Interstate 43. He cranked up the radio and willed himself to think of Puerto Rico and the upcoming photo assignment. Gold had lured Christopher Columbus, Francis Drake, and Dutch mariners to that historic island hundreds of years ago. But it was the golden opportunity of outrunning his thoughts that spurred him on.

Having an hour at his disposal, Seth bowed to rare impulse and turned his film in at the airport one-hour shop instead of waiting to develop it himself. He watched the pictures come off the belt and down the chute. One in particular captured his attention— Kayla, holding the baby, her expression unguarded. As always, it was her eyes that leaped out at him.

A suitable caption completely failed him. Not that it needed one. The longing in those lovely green eyes said it all. Art and antiques might be filling her spare time, and maybe she *did* want the postmaster job. But she wanted a child more. He sat down, almost sick with the emotions sweeping over him.

Despite the years, the distance in miles, the lack of communication, he'd hung onto her in his heart. It was a fantasy, of course, to believe that she'd always be there. A selfish fantasy. Life went on. For her, as well as for him.

It was Farrell in her life now. Facts were facts, there to be faced. Why did he feel a grayness closing in? A resistance to what was there?

Because, by nature, he was competitive? A sore loser? Or had he only just realized he'd never stopped loving her? Even as Seth rejected the thought, he was remembering the early days—her zest for life, her thoughtfulness, her sensitivity, even her quaintness—how appealing she'd been.

The years had not changed who she was. Rather, time had honed and enriched her most precious qualities just as it had deepened his appreciation for them.

Seth paid the clerk, took the packet of pictures, and sat down to wait for his flight to be announced. He thumbed through the pictures rapidly, so blindly that he almost overlooked the one he'd taken that very morning as he'd awaited his rental car.

It was a shot of a Japanese dignitary climbing out of a stretch limo. He'd taken the picture, not because he'd recognized the fellow—he hadn't—rather, because in his business, one often took pictures and got the details later. It was the sort of picture that had, in the past, developed into freelance articles. In this case, it paid a dividend of different sorts. Seth had inadvertently caught Richard Farrell and his lady friend in the shot. They'd passed directly in front of the camera.

The woman on Richard's arm was a tall, willowy blond. Late twenties. Her fur coat hung open. Stylish attire accessorized with expensive-looking jewelry contributed to her cosmopolitan bearing. There was an air of intimacy in the smile she and Richard exchanged.

Seth studied the picture a long time, attentive to every detail. This wasn't a simple business acquaintance, he was pretty sure of that. And if by some long stretch of the imagination she was just a friend—well, what harm would it do to send the photo to Kayla? Anonymously, of course.

It seemed self-serving. Cruel, in a way. Yet if Farrell was deceiving her, didn't she deserve to know? Seth wrestled with himself a full hour before relieving himself of the difficult decision. He mailed the picture to Josh.

four

Kayla made it to church in time for Sunday school. Richard, clean-shaven and smelling of a spicy cologne, joined her later for morning worship. She enjoyed the blend of voices lifted in songs of praise and the uplifting message that followed.

As the final strains of the postlude faded away, Kayla followed Richard out of the pew. She took the arm he offered and smiled, saying, "I fixed a casserole and salad to take to Shelly's for lunch. Why don't you join us?"

"Sorry, Kayla. Not today," said Richard.

"Are you sure? You still haven't seen the baby."

"Misha's fixing something. She'll be going back to school later this afternoon and won't be coming home again until spring break," Richard added. "I want to spend a little time with her."

Though Misha's response to Kayla had never been warm, Kayla respected Richard's devotion to his daughter. Swallowing her disappointment, she followed him to the back of the sanctuary where he helped her into her coat.

"Where's your green scarf?" Richard asked.

Color rose to Kayla's cheeks, for he'd given her the scarf for Christmas. "Seth forgot to return it

47

before he left," she admitted. "He will, though. He's just a bit absent-minded."

Though he looked unhappy about it, Richard said nothing more about the scarf. As they stood waiting to shake hands with the minister, he smoothed down her collar. "After Misha leaves for school, I've got some book work to do. But if I get finished on time, I'll pick you up for Bible study. How's that sound?"

"That'd be nice." Kayla smiled and hid her surprise, for it was his first show of interest in the Bible study group. "The group just finished the book of Romans. Jerry Carlisle's a terrific teacher."

They parted company in the church parking lot. Kayla drove home, changed clothes, and took her casserole and salad to Shelly's house. Joshua and Brent helped put the meal on the table while Shelly caught up on some much-needed rest. After lunch, Kayla played games with Brent and visited with Joshua and Shelly. Late in the afternoon, Kayla Joy awoke from her nap, and fussed until Brent lost all patience.

"Can't a guy get a piece of quiet around here?" he demanded, his little round face stamped in indignation.

Kayla found it hard not to laugh with both Shelly and Joshua fighting smiles. She hugged Brent and kissed the top of his head. "Tell you what—let's go get a pizza."

"Just you and me?" he asked, and Kayla nodded.

"Maybe by the time we get back with it, Little

Joy'll be purring like a kitten," said Kayla.

The thought of his baby sister purring tickled Brent's funny bone. He chased down his coat and boots while Kayla phoned for the pizza. At the Pizza Pit, they met Misha coming out as they were going in.

"Misha! Hi! I thought you'd be on your way back to school by now," Kayla said, pausing in the open door.

The shapely coed tossed her tawny head. "Change of plans. I'm going to get up early and drive back in the morning. I've gotta run. We both skipped lunch, and Dad's starving!"

So Misha hadn't fixed lunch after all. Kayla chewed her bottom lip, thinking of her earlier invitation. Richard may as well have eaten with them! His lack of interest in spending time with those close to her was disappointing.

"Aunt Kayla? Can we get bread sticks, too?"

Tugged out of her reverie, Kayla smiled agreement. The baby was still fussing when they returned. Kayla ate a quick bite, then rocked her while Shelly ate. Kayla Joy fell asleep in Kayla's arms. She tucked her tenderly into her cradle, then hurried home to freshen up for Bible study.

But when the appointed hour came, Richard didn't show. Kayla resisted the urge to phone him and went alone. In the beginning, she'd attended out of a sense of doing what was right rather than a hunger for understanding the Scriptures. Yet as her involvement in the prison ministry had deepened, she'd seen the absolute necessity of being grounded in God's Word. No way could she field difficult and sometimes bitter questions flung at her from people whose broken lives screamed out for a Savior. The discussions, the prayer, and the sharing that went on in that small group of Christian friends was food for her soul. She drove home, inspired by the session and disappointed that Richard hadn't shared in it.

The phone was ringing when Kayla walked in the door of her apartment. Almost certain it would be Richard, she was surprised to hear Seth's voice.

"Seth! What's up? I thought you were in Puerto Rico!"

"I am. It's gorgeous here. A little too warm for your scarf, though. Had you missed it yet?"

"Only my neck."

He laughed. "Remember that piece of sage advice, 'Never a borrower or lender be?'"

Kayla chuckled and slipped out of her coat and shoes. She pulled her feet up under her and rested the phone in her lap. "I like a well-traveled scarf. Will it come back to me stamped like a passport?"

"I can't promise you that, but I will do my best not to misplace it between now and Friday."

"Friday?"

"Unless something else comes up, I'll be in Kitterly on Friday. I'll return it then. Or would you rather I dropped it in the mail?"

"No, that's not necessary. So what'd you leave at

Josh and Shelly's that you can't do without?"

Seth managed to sound injured. "Can't I come visit my family without your thinking I'm hunting down lost articles?"

"Two weekends in a row? I don't think so."

"And here I was going to give you one more chance to come along on the Route 66 shoot!"

"Must have been your favorite camera."

"Listen to you!" He chuckled. "Actually, I thought Shelly might be feeling more like company by Friday. Josh and I can have a real visit, and I'll bring Brent some more shells. How about passing the word along for me?"

"I'd be happy to."

"Great! Maybe I'll see you then. If not, I'll leave the scarf with Shelly."

"That's fine."

Seth paused a moment, then asked, "Everything okay?"

It came out of the blue, his concern. Startled, Kayla said, "Just fine. How about you?"

"Fine here, too." Sounding more like himself, he brought the call to a close, saying, "Guess I'd better hit the sheets, I've got a shoot at sunrise."

"Good luck. It was nice of you to call, Seth," she added, before bidding him goodbye.

Kayla puzzled over the call as she ran her bath water. There for a moment, he'd sounded almost worried. As if there were more he'd like to say, but didn't quite know how. That wasn't like Seth! He was seldom at a loss for words. Catching herself making too much of too little, Kayla padded into the bathroom and filled the tub.

She eased into the warm, fragrant bubbles, settled back, and closed her eyes. Her thoughts flitted back to Saturday. Her heart had nearly stopped when she looked up to see Seth in the doorway of the nursery. Like a child nursing a skinned knee, she had, upon seeing him again, instinctively braced herself for the ripping away of the bandage, the exposure of the raw wound. But once the shock had faded and they'd spent time together, her pulse had slowed, her heartbeat steadied. Even Seth's parting kiss had not shaken her.

She was shouting happy about that. God, she realized, had healed her hurt with His tender care. His covenant with her, made when she accepted Christ as her Lord, came with a blessing—His unfailing love and commitment to her wholeness. Covenant. After tonight's study, the word had deeper meaning.

A covenant, Jerry Carlisle had explained to the study group, came with both blessing and curse. The blessing was realized when the covenant was kept, the curse when it was broken. Jerry had used the modern-day illustration of marriage to describe a covenant. Kayla had grasped that explanation readily, for she saw in her sister's marriage the blessing of love and peace and joy. She hoped for that special covenant someday, too.

As Kayla toweled off, pulled on her nightgown, and slipped beneath the covers, she wondered if Richard was a man with whom a life-long covenant could be kept. The rosy glow of excitement she'd felt for Seth seven years ago was missing in her relationship with Richard, but she was more mature now, less given to yo-yo extremes of emotion. She enjoyed Richard's company. They shared common interests. He was attentive, generous, and a family man, as evidenced by his devotion to Misha.

Kayla's eyelids drooped as she lingered in the hazy corridor between wakefulness and sleep, pondering the little things. She wished Richard would show more interest in getting to know her family! It flitted through her mind, too, that it would have been nice if he'd been a little less childish about Seth. Or was that expecting too much? Kayla fell asleep without arriving at a conclusion.

The next morning Kayla bundled up and walked to work. She'd put up all the first class and was working through a stack of newspapers when the postmaster, Charlie Gaines, unlocked the service window.

"Morning, Richard. Cold enough for you?" she heard Charlie greet their first customer of the day.

"It's brisk, all right. Can't last long, with spring just around the corner. Kayla back there?"

"Right here." Kayla crossed to the window and gave Richard a little wave.

"I'll let you wait on this fella." Charlie winked at her and lumbered back to the presort case.

Richard stamped the snow off his wingtips and smiled. "How's my little treasure this morning?"

"Pretty busy, so far. First class mail's all up and I'm working on *Weekly Gazettes*." She shoved her hands, black with printer's ink, into her smock pockets and hoped Richard hadn't noticed. His wool coat hung open, revealing a spotless suit, a crisply pressed white shirt, and a perfectly knotted tie. He pushed a numbered yellow slip across the counter.

"Looks as if you have something for me."

"Certified letter." Kayla withdrew it from a slot crowded with certifieds. She noted, in handing it to him, that it was from the Internal Revenue Service. Noticed too, to her chagrin, that she'd left a black thumb print in one corner.

"I'm sorry about not making it to Bible study last night." Richard paused in signing the numbered yellow slip, pulled a wry face, and added, "I'd fallen behind on some tax forms. I lost all track of time. It was nine o'clock before I knew it!"

Kayla knew from her chance meeting with Misha that that wasn't quite true. She put the yellow slip to one side and tore the green return receipt off the back of the letter, saying quietly, "You missed a good study. Sign line five, please."

They visited until another customer came in, requiring Kayla's attention. It was a busy morning that followed. Kayla went home for a sandwich at noon. Richard called her just as she was ready to return to work.

"This is sort of embarrassing, but I need a favor," he said.

"Oh? What's that?" Kayla propped the phone against her shoulder and dried her hands.

"That yellow slip I signed this morning—what do you do with that?"

"File it. Why?"

"If the IRS should call the post office and ask, you have a record of my having received the letter?" he asked.

"Yes. But they won't have to call. They'll know you received the letter when they get the green return receipt card with your signature on it," she pointed out. "Why?"

"Could you destroy them both? The yellow slip and the green return card?"

"Richard, I can't do that!" said Kayla, alarmed that he'd ask.

"What's the big deal? If they don't get the card back, they'll assume it was lost in the mail and send me another one. That's plausible, isn't it?"

"I suppose. Though it's more likely they'll assume you simply refused acceptance," said Kayla, still reeling from his request. "Not that it matters. I won't do it."

"They're pressuring me for money I don't owe! I need time to drag out last year's records, get in touch with my old bookkeeper, and talk to an attorney. Otherwise, I don't have much hope of a judgment coming in my favor." His voice turned cajoling as he added, "All I want is to buy a little time. Is that asking so much?"

"I'm sorry, Richard. I can't help you."

"No one would ever know."

"I'm obligated to provide the service purchased by the sender." Kayla remained firm.

An awkward silence followed, broken finally by Richard's sigh. "All right, no harm in asking. Bye-bye, my little goody-two-shoes."

Blood rushed to Kayla's face as she hung up the phone. She returned to work and tried to finish out the afternoon without betraying her emotions, but a sense of shattered peace haunted her. No matter how she viewed it, what Richard had asked was dishonest!

After work, Kayla ate a solitary meal in her efficiency kitchen, then called her sister.

"If he has a dispute with the IRS, why isn't he ironing it out instead of playing cat and mouse?" asked Shelly, after hearing her out.

"The IRS isn't always right," Kayla said swiftly, then flushed, realizing how defensive she sounded. She sighed. "I'm not trying to justify his request. I guess I'm still kind of shocked and looking for an explanation.

"Maybe you don't know Richard as well as you think you do," murmured Shelly.

Maybe Shelly was right. Maybe she didn't! Kayla knew his taste in clothes and cars and food. She could wander through a flea market and know at a glance which items would interest him. And she knew his views on politics and education and all that was wrong with the country. But what did those views say about who Richard really was? Kayla spent a restless night and dragged to work the next morning on limbs that ached with weariness.

At eight-thirty, she slipped out of the smock protecting her white-washed denim jumper and unlocked the service window. Richard was waiting for her.

"Good morning," he said, and she responded.

But her palms grew moist, and she had a hard time meeting his gaze because of the matter that hung between them. Each waited for the other to bring attention to it.

Richard bought several stamps. The awkward silence grew as he affixed them to letters. Just when Kayla thought he was going to leave with no mention of yesterday, he said quietly, "The IRS is a little intimidating. I panicked, plain and simple, and I'm sorry." His gaze entreated understanding.

"You're feeling better about it today, then?" Kayla asked cautiously.

"After talking to my tax man, yes!"

"Good."

"Forgive me?" he asked.

She nodded and tried to smile, but the knot in her stomach had yet to dissolve.

"I've got another little problem. Don't worry—it's nothing to test your scruples."

"Richard!" she protested.

He grimaced and said, "Sorry. That wasn't intended as criticism. I respect your scruples, like them in fact."

She lowered her lashes, questioning whether or not he shared those values.

"The sump pump quit working in the basement, and I've got to be out of town for a few days," Richard continued. "The snow's melting and I'm afraid, with the pump broken, I'm going to have a water problem. Rather than risk damaging some valuable old pieces, I wondered if you'd mind my moving the antiques out of my basement and into your shop."

"That's fine with me, Richard."

"I'll get the pump fixed and my things out of your way just as soon as I get back," Richard promised.

Kayla sorted through her keys, found the one to the depot, and took it off the ring. "I've got a spare at home. You can hang onto this one until you get home."

Richard visited a moment longer, then leaned across the counter to land a kiss on her cheek. Kayla returned to putting up mail. She worked quickly and accurately, but her thoughts were miles away from the pieces of mail flying from her hand to the boxes. She didn't mind Richard storing a few things in the depot. He could fill it to overflowing, and she wouldn't complain. But she still felt trouble over the certified letter. She prayed concerning the matter and continued to do so as the week progressed.

Richard called on Wednesday to say he missed her. Kayla was about to echo similar feelings when she recognized it was relief, rather than regret that she was feeling. She needed time and space to explore her heart and head.

On Thursday, Kayla got a postcard from Puerto Rico. It pictured a sunset spilling purple rays across placid tropical waters. Seth's handwriting, never anything to brag about, had deteriorated over the past few years. She finally made out the scrawled message. *Pack your bags and don't forget your brushes!* Smiling, she turned the card over. Obviously, she'd given Seth the wrong impression about her art lessons. This was a sunset only God could paint!

The mail was heavier than usual on Friday. Kayla threw her own mail to one side as she sorted. But it was after lunch before she got around to opening it. There was the electric bill, a newsletter from a mission she supported, and a plain white envelope with no return address.

As she slit the envelope open, a picture fell out. In the foreground was Richard with a woman who looked as if she'd stepped right off the cover of some slick woman's magazine. Dark glasses and a fashionable hat lent an air of mystery to the statuesque, exquisitely attired stranger.

Kayla stared at the snapshot, recoiling as if from a blow. Who was she? Why was she with Richard? A business acquaintance? No, the smile they exchanged had an intimate quality. She was clinging to his arm. Possessively. Kayla flashed hot and cold, her stomach lurching.

"Kayla? You've got a customer at the window," called the postmaster.

Kayla bolted to attention. She stuffed the picture into her jumper pocket and hurried to the counter where a tall, barrel-shaped man waited.

He scratched his bald dome. "I'm looking for a guy named Richard Farrell. Can you tell me where he lives?"

Richard, everywhere she turned! Kayla's pulse leaped as her gaze swept over the man. His business suit was well-cut, his tie conservative. She'd met so few of Richard's business associates. This man didn't look familiar.

Handling his request by the book, she said, "I'm sorry, sir. I'm not allowed to give out street addresses."

The man's fleshy face reddened with impatience. "I'm with the Department of Revenue, Miss, and I'd appreciate a little cooperation. I don't believe I caught your name."

Kayla was about to ask for some ID when Shelly's neighbor burst into the lobby, her child wailing in her arms. "Excuse me, Kayla. I'm sorry to interrupt, but Tommy fell in the lobby. Have you got a tissue or something?"

Kayla passed her a tissue. The little boy, trying to avoid having his bleeding nose wiped, reared back in his mother's arms. The flailing motion spattered blood on his mother, on the counter, and on Kayla's hand.

Kayla closed her eyes and tried to brace herself against the counter before the grayness closed in. Her effort was too little, too late. She felt herself sinking into darkness, floating beneath the surface. Her last conscious thought was of the customer and her unlocked cash drawer. The next thing she knew, the postmaster, Charlie Gaines, was bending over her.

"Kayla! That a girl. Open your eyes. Shake it off. The kid's gone now. I mopped up the counter. Come on, you can open your eyes now."

Charlie's leathery face came into focus. Strength flowed once more to Kayla's limbs, and with his help, she got to her feet. It wasn't the first time she'd fainted at the sight of blood, far from it. On rare occasion, she could cling by a thread and overpower the faintness. But not this time. Perhaps it had been jolt upon jolt—the stranger asking for Richard right on the heels of the picture, then the blood.

Realizing the stranger was gone, she thought once again of her cash drawer. It was instinctive, the quick check to make certain she hadn't been robbed. Everything seemed to be in order.

"Here, sit down." Charlie pushed the desk chair into position.

Kayla protested, "I'm okay now."

"No, you're not. You're white as that pile of snow

out the window. Now sit!" he said sternly. "I'll watch the counter."

"Charlie, I'm fine! Really."

"Then you do a sit-down job. The rural delivery report's waiting. The safety report, too. And when you get done with that, you can close out your drawer and do the books."

Charlie was trying to be kind. But figures weren't Kayla's strong point. Her unsettled state of mind didn't help matters any. She poked a column of numbers into the adding machine and stared at it, unseeingly. Who was the woman with Richard? Where was the picture taken? And why was it sent to her? The postmark was local, the address, typewritten. *Misha!*

Whether or not it was Misha who'd sent the picture, one thing was clear—the picture was very recent. She'd been with Richard when he'd bought that coat a little over two weeks ago. Shelly's earlier statement echoed in her ears. How well *did* she know Richard? Did she know him at all?

"Are you stuck?" asked Charlie, peeking over her shoulder.

Realizing she'd been staring into space for a good long while, Kayla flushed and murmured, "Sorry. I was wool gathering." She started hitting keys again as her confidence in the man she'd been dating for the past few months completely unraveled.

five

At five o'clock, Charlie took down the flag, locked up the front lobby, and told Kayla to go home and start enjoying her vacation. Kayla realized with a jolt that she hadn't, in the past few hours, thought at all about the two weeks of free time looming ahead.

While Charlie lugged the out-going mail sacks to the cart in the back room, she combed wisps of hair back from her face with ink-smudged fingers and slipped her coat on over her white-washed denim jumper.

The back door of the post office opened into a snow-slushed alley. There was a motor home parked between Kayla and the street beyond. Just as she came even with it, the door flew open and a familiar figure stepped out. She stopped short.

"Seth!"

"You look surprised. I told you I'd be in Kitterly on Friday."

"I guess you did." Kayla combed a hand through disheveled hair and admitted, "I wasn't thinking. This day's been unreal!"

Seth's blue eyes swept her face. Concern darkened his gaze. "Want to talk about it?"

Humiliate herself by revealing Richard's duplic-

ity? She shook her head. "No, thanks."

Seth stuffed fingertips into the pockets of his faded jeans, hunched his shoulders against the breeze, and regarded her a moment longer. "You sure? Sometimes it helps to unload."

"That's nice, but no." Abruptly, Kayla changed the subject. "Did you spend the day with Josh?"

"Until a while ago. He's working second shift," Seth explained. "I took some pictures of Brent holding Kayla Joy. I think she's grown just since last weekend."

"They're calling her Joy," Kayla murmured.

"It's Kayla Joy to me. She'll just have to get used to her eccentric uncle."

"I've never thought of you as being eccentric. Individualistic, maybe."

"Fine line." Seth's white grin emphasized the deepness of his tan. He indicated his motor home with a wave of the hand. "What do you think of my toy?"

Kayla's gaze traveled the sleek lines of the motor home. "Brand-spanking new, isn't it?"

"Pretty much so." He glanced at the empty drive and asked, "Did you walk to work?"

Kayla nodded.

"Hop in, and I'll give you a ride home. It's quite an outfit. There's a bedroom. A bathroom too, though, at the moment, it's doubling as a dark room."

The modest-sized interior had that new-car smell. The color scheme, a tasteful coordination of buff and country blue with occasional strokes of deep rose, was both restful and pleasing to the eye. There was a wide bunk up over the cab, a dining booth, and a tiny kitchen space with all the creature comforts.

Kayla found it warm and inviting and surprisingly neat for a man who used to have some rather untidy habits. Her green scarf was folded neatly in the passenger's seat, a plush captain's chair that swiveled. She wandered back to the bedroom. The bed and built-in counter and drawers were littered with luggage, books, maps, and a laptop computer. Now, this was the sort of loosely-organized clutter she'd anticipated!

"A traveling office as well as a home away from home," said Kayla with a smile. "Very nice."

"I've lived out of a suitcase for years. This'll take some getting used to. Have you ever driven one of these things?" Seth asked, leading the way to the front.

"No."

"She rides like a dream. Here, give it a try." He beckoned toward the seat.

Bowing to his boyish enthusiasm, Kayla peeled off her coat and sat down in the driver's seat. Her gaze darted about as she familiarized herself with the shift column, the instrument panel, the brake, and accelerator.

"Was there an incident at the post office today, or did you cut yourself shaving?" Seth interrupted her concentration. He grinned and indicated her blouse.

Kayla peered into the mirror at the dark stain on her collar. Dried blood lacked the punch of fresh. She shuddered, but only lightly. "A little boy fell and bloodied his nose this afternoon."

"Uh-oh. Did you. . .?"

"Right on cue." Kayla rolled her eyes and Seth grinned. "I didn't realize he was bleeding, or I wouldn't have looked."

"Remind me never to come to you for medical attention. Fasten your seat belt, and that'll quit," Seth added above the loud buzzing noise that began the moment she turned the key.

Kayla snapped the seat belt into place and was rewarded with silence. "I'm fine with bruises, bumps, and broken bones. Just don't bleed on me. What's so funny?"

Seth's blue eyes twinkled with suppressed laughter. "I was remembering our first movie. I thought you'd gone to sleep. Your head was resting against me. Real cozy! The credits rolled, I gave you a nudge, and you slumped right out of the seat."

Kayla flushed. Easing the gear shift into reverse, she asked, "You sure you trust me to back this thing out?"

"Limp as a rag," he went on, still grinning. "Scared me to death!"

"Served you right. That movie, as I recall, had enough blood in it to make a surgeon squeamish! Am I missing the burn barrel? Take a peek, would you?"

Seth ceased his teasing and guided Kayla down

the alley. She backed into the street, then rolled down Main Street right past the sheriff's office. Josh was out in front, cleaning off the windows of his patrol car.

Kayla beeped the horn. Josh grinned and waved. Seth beamed encouragement. "You're getting the hang of it. If you're in no hurry to get home, give it a try on the open road."

Kayla turned right and left Kitterly behind. The tenseness within, the numbness, the wounded voice that pleaded a logical explanation, receded a bit as she followed the country road between melting banks of snow. The sun bled orange and pink across the western horizon as a flock of geese beat wings against the fading sky. She drew a deep breath and let it out slowly.

Seth's chatter about horsepower, RPMs, and gas mileage insulated her against the torment that had dogged her beginning the moment that picture of Richard had fallen out of the envelope! But the reprieve, she knew, couldn't last forever. She had a lot of thinking to do. Richard might come home tonight. Or call. She had to be ready. As twilight faded, Kayla turned around in a farmer's driveway and headed back to town.

The street lights had come on by the time she parked along the curb in front of her apartment. "Thanks, Seth. That was fun. It's a nice piece of machinery." Kayla slipped out of the driver's seat and shrugged into her coat.

Seth rose, too. He returned her green scarf,

teasing, "Bet you thought I'd lose it in Puerto Rico, didn't you?"

"It wouldn't have been the end of the world if you had." She tried to smile as she moved toward the door. "Thanks for the lift, Seth."

"Wait a second. Before you go, give me one more chance to talk you into coming along on the Route 66 shoot. If you don't mind my saying so, I think it'd do you good," he added.

Kayla looked at him in surprise. "What do you mean?"

"You're tired. A real vacation could be just what the doctor ordered."

She curbed a defensive reply and said evenly, "I have two weeks to catch up on my rest."

"You won't, though. Not if you stay here in Kitterly," he said. "Shelly's bragged all day about what a help you've been, carrying in meals, spending time with Brent, rocking the baby, doing the laundry. Sounds to me like you're doing a great job of taking care of everyone but Kayla Colter."

"Shelly had a rough pregnancy. She needed a little help. Besides, spending time with Brent and little Joy is no hardship. I've enjoyed myself," Kayla added. "It wasn't work, it was play!"

Seth jutted out his jaw. "Then I'd say you're about played out. You need to rock back and take it easy for a spell."

He was right, but not for any of the reasons he'd mentioned. Kayla was confused, heart-sore, questioning her instincts.

Seth reached out and tipped up her chin with a gentle touch. He searched her face a long moment, then said softly, "Can't have a sweet girl like you losing her sparkle, now can we? Come on, say you'll come. There's nothing like traveling with a filming crew to take your mind off your problems."

To Kayla's horror, tears pricked the back of her eyes. Ordinarily, her feelings weren't that close to the surface. But Seth's concern, coming on the heels of the day she'd just spent, touched a nerve. Thankful she'd shut off the motor, throwing the interior of the motor home in darkness, she moved away from him, fumbled for the door handle, and let herself out.

"Kayla?" Seth called, surprise ringing in his voice.

"Thanks for the ride, Seth." She flung a hand in the air but kept going, gaining speed, just making the door to her apartment before the tears spilled free.

Her cheeks were damp as she kicked off her shoes and shed her coat. She padded barefoot across the cold tile, furniture blurring before her eyes. Plucking a tissue from the box on the end table, Kayla curled up on the sofa and cried it out.

As tear storms go, it was brief. Nothing at all like what she'd gone through after her broken engagement with Seth. That was different, though. She'd loved Seth much more. The realization brought her up short. She examined it more closely and found it to be accurate. She *had* loved Seth more. She'd survived that, with God's help, and life had eventually become meaningful again. She'd survive this, too.

But for the moment, she was numb. She'd thought Richard was devoted to her. Perhaps more devoted, even, than she was to him. She'd wanted to be devoted—wanted their relationship to work, to deepen, to grow into a lasting commitment. She'd prayed that it would.

No, she'd prayed for God's guidance, she corrected herself.

Kayla let that thought settle in. God's guidance. Part of the covenant He'd made with her. She bowed her head in the midst of tears and tattered tissues and let the words of a favorite Psalm gentle her wounded spirit: "He who dwells in the shelter of the Most High, will rest in the shadow of the Almighty. I will say of the Lord, He is my refuge and fortress, My God in whom I trust!"

A soothing peace followed on the heels of prayer. Kayla pulled the afghan over her, closed her eyes, and slept like a baby.

Kayla awoke at three in the morning. She showered and washed and styled her hair. Jeans, cable-knit sweater, and a favorite pair of sneakers comforted her with their familiarity. She made herself a cup of tea and reached for her Bible. At five, she closed it and prayed once again. Then she picked up the phone, called Shelly's house, and asked for Seth.

His voice came over the line almost immediately. "Kayla? What's up?"

He sounded wide awake. Kayla took a deep breath, winged one last prayer, and asked, "Does your invitation still stand?"

"You mean you want to come along?" Surprise rang in his voice.

"That's right. What time are we leaving?"

"As soon as you can be ready. I'm supposed to be in Chicago at nine."

Thankful he hadn't complicated the matter with a lot of questions, Kayla said, "Give me ten minutes."

She flew to the bedroom, dragged out a suitcase, and was ready in seven-and-a-half minutes.

As they took the interstate south, Seth kept shooting Kayla sidelong glances. She had a feeling he couldn't quite believe she'd come. The homebody bit of her couldn't believe it, either.

After a bit, he asked, "Does Richard know his little treasure's leaving town?"

"No. And if you don't mind, I'd rather not talk about Richard. As for that little treasure business—"

"Nauseating," he said, cheeky enough to grin.

"Forget it, okay?" said Kayla.

"Fine with me."

Little treasure—what an irony! Kayla stared out the window. The dark countryside sped past her window. Seth turned on the radio and tuned in an easy-listening station. Kayla closed her eyes. The music washed over her, soft and soothing. Milwaukee came and went. Lack of sleep caught up with her. She pulled her coat up around her shoulders and slept the rest of the way to Chicago.

six

They arrived in the windy city with time to spare. Seth exited onto Lake Shore Drive and made a sweep through Grant Park just as the sun broke through the pall of exhaust fumes rising from the busy streets. Despite the sunshine, the city was living up to it's name. Blasts of glacial air whipped the waters of Lake Michigan and swept across the winter-bleached park, scattering dead leaves and debris.

"That's the Art Institute," said Seth, in passing.

Kayla admired the noble stone lions flanking the entrance. A block farther on, patches of gray snow lingered in the shadow of Buckingham Fountain. Shedd Aquarium, Field Museum of Natural History, and Adler Planetarium—names she'd heard all her life—suddenly took shape: solid, dignified edifices aged by winds and seasons and the wear of countless visitors.

"Living within a few of hours of these places, yet never having taken advantage of them makes me ashamed of myself," Kayla admitted as they made their way to Jackson Street.

Seth grinned. "Say, I like the sound of that. Could make a gypsy out of you yet." Encouraged by her smile, he added, "Tell you what—let's get

Josh and Shelly and the kids to come, and we'll make a long weekend of it one of these days. Brent's a little young for some of the spots, but he'd love Shedd Aquarium. You've got to see it to believe the variety of fish under one roof!"

Kayla let the invitation pass without comment. On the heels of Richard's duplicity, she mistrusted herself, mistrusted, too, the sharp awareness Seth's close proximity was triggering. In her haste to be out of Kitterly and what remained to be faced there, she hadn't considered the intimacy of shared travel. Miss Williams and her crew would be a welcome intrusion.

Deftly changing the subject, Kayla said, "This note-taking business could do with a bit of explaining. How am I to know what's noteworthy?"

"Mostly, I need a catalog of pictures as I take them. Who's in them, any pertinent information."

"Where's my tablet?"

"We'll have to pick one up along the way."

Seth's offhand manner, as he parked the motor home near a popular breakfast spot and reached for his camera, made Kayla wonder if he'd only suggested notetaking to make her feel as if she were earning her keep on this trip.

Whatever his reasons for inviting her along, Kayla couldn't fault his hospitality. The food in the Jackson Street eatery was scrumptious, the atmosphere delightful. Seth's enthusiasm for the trip ahead made for easy conversation.

"Restaurants like this are part of the highway's

allure," Seth said, smiling at Kayla as he drained his cup. "Family-owned restaurants dotted the whole route when it was the main east-west artery. Of course, you never knew until the food was in front of you just what sort of treat you were in for."

"Or trick," said the gray-haired waitress, having overheard Seth's comment as she slipped up to fill his coffee cup. Crevices deepened around her droll mouth. "I could name you a few mom and pop operations where the cuisine sure enough seemed more a trick than a treat!"

"Most of us could," agreed Seth with a grin. Good-naturedly, he added, "But, when you turned off the road, you knew where you were. Nowadays, take the off ramp of any interstate in America and everything looks the same. Motels, shopping malls, fast food chains."

The waitress's double chin quivered as she cackled and slid the check onto the table. "I know your kind, you're one of them two-lane highway buffs!"

"Get a lot of those, do you?" asked Seth.

"Route Sixty-sixers? You bet. Right out there on the corner of Michigan Avenue and Jackson Street is where the highway began." She indicated the direction with a wave of the coffee pot. "They come in here like they was on a religious pilgrimage or something. Seems to me they're having a lot more fun remembering than anyone ever had driving on that old narrow slab of a road. I'll take the interstate any day!"

Seth grinned and owned up to belonging to that

peculiar brotherhood that held the 66 in affectionate esteem. He introduced Kayla and himself.

"May. May Rybarth." The waitress set the coffee pot down and gave first Seth's, then Kayla's hand a firm grip.

When Seth explained their project and asked permission to take her picture, May expressed regret that the owner wasn't available to talk with them. She suggested they might like to arrange a meeting with him, then after a token protest, smiled into Seth's camera.

"We were here before they built the highway. Or so they tell me—that was a little before my time." May grinned as Seth recapped his lens.

Kayla scrambled in her pocketbook for a scrap of paper on which to take notes. "If the travelers were always this well fed, they probably didn't have to eat again until they wheeled through Kansas," she said as she scribbled May's name on the back of an envelope.

"You had to get a good meal under your belt if you were going any distance. There's one thing that hasn't changed! Folks still come in here and fuel up before heading west."

Kayla's pen flew as May provided what information she could concerning the restaurant before trotting off to fill coffee cups at the next table.

Seth excused himself to pay the check. Jessica Williams, who was to host the travel feature, and her film crew of one came in while he was at the register. Dressed in black, with dark hair neatly swept back from an Ivory-girl face, the anchorwoman cut a striking figure. She acknowledged Seth's introduction of Kayla with a brief smile and a businesslike handshake.

"This is my camera-audio man Mark Gibbons." Miss Williams introduced an unshaven young man with raging red hair.

Gibbons acknowledged Kayla with a brief nod, then shook Seth's hand, saying, "I enjoyed your book, Mr. Brooks."

"Thanks. That's always nice to hear. And by the way, it's just Seth. No need for formalities among fellow road warriors." Seth included Miss Williams in his smile. "Everyone comfortable with that?"

Kayla and Mark nodded agreement.

"Fine, fine," said Jessica, her thoughts clearly on the job ahead. She slipped into the chair Seth pulled out for her.

Seth joined Mark and the ladies at the table. He consulted Jessica, asking, "What do you think of shooting some film here? The waitress tells me it's been in the same family since it's opening. Unfortunately, the owner isn't around today."

"In that case, why don't Mark and I come back when we return to the city next week?" suggested Jessica.

"Sounds good," agreed Seth.

"As you know, my staff has made a number of phone calls, arranging interviews with some of the establishments you suggested along the route. I finalized the schedule after talking with you last week." Jessica slipped on a pair of eyeglasses and passed a printed itinerary to Seth.

Seth scanned it briefly. "St. Louis by nightfall? That's pretty ambitious. I'd liked to spend some time chatting with local folks along the way. They can lead you to things you'd never find on your own."

"That's all very well and good when time isn't an issue. However, in this case, I'm afraid we'll fall hopelessly behind if we don't stick closely to our schedule," Jessica replied in a pleasant, yet authoritative voice.

Kayla could see, even as Seth graciously let it go, that he wasn't entirely in agreement with the well-organized news anchor. Jessica whipped out her own copy of the itinerary and detailed what she expected to be the highlights of the day. May brought more coffee and Mark's order.

Mark made short work of his breakfast, then excused himself to get the necessary equipment for their first shoot. It was to be on the nearby corner where an updated placard had replaced the original 66 sign which had come down in 1977. Seth, Kayla, and Jessica soon caught up with him. Clad in denims gone thin at the elbows and knees, Mark shivered as he set up the shot, then leaned over the tripod and gave Jessica her signal.

Experience lending ease and composure, she led in by pointing out the sign which read, "Here began Route 66."

"Sixty-six, the highway America loved best, has been immortalized in literature, in song, and in a television series bearing its name. It began right here at Chicago in 1926. Route 66 snaked westward, linking the midwestern prairies to the hills and plains and desert of the southwest, ending finally at the Pacific Ocean.

"It was known affectionately as the hard road, the Mother Road, the Main Street of America. And it was indeed the main street of the countless small towns and cities through which passed a steady stream of the nation's freighters, dreamers, and restless spirits. Though the last section of road was decommissioned a decade ago, this sign commemorating the once great highway is a testimony to the heartbeat of memory, of affection, of esteem. What fickle creatures we are. Yearning for bigger and better, yet wistfully reaching back for what we have, in the headlong rush, cast aside."

"Right on," Seth said softly. His thumb came up, signaling approval as Jessica wound to a close her well-prepared invitation for the viewers to sit back and cruise along the old highway of memories.

Looking on as Seth snapped a picture of the sign, Kayla smiled, knowing suddenly why this project appealed to him. It was the dreamer in him. The romantic. The side of his nature she'd loved most dearly.

Unexpectedly, he turned and gave her hand a squeeze. Smiling, he said, "I'm glad you came."

Kayla returned the pressure. She was glad, too,

even as she slipped her hand free. Glad for the shared moment, for the day ahead, for the distraction it provided, freeing her to hold tangled thoughts of Richard at bay.

Mark stashed the equipment in the company van. Jessica instructed him to follow them to the Rialto theatre, a Route 66 landmark in the prison town of Joliet, while Seth and Kayla ducked into a nearby shop and bought a notebook.

Giving up the front passenger's seat to Jessica, Kayla settled into the dining nook of the motor home. The frantic traffic of the Loop spilled them onto Ogden Avenue, which, according to Seth, had once been the City 66, the business route. Ogden angled west and gently south through the suburbs of Cicero, Al Capone's center of operations back in the days of when mobsters ruled the mean South Side of Chicago.

Kayla's interest quickened as they passed an array of railroad switching yards so extensive that her little antique shop depot would have looked like a child's toy set out in the middle of all that steel track. Seth pulled over and snapped a few pictures while Kayla scribbled brief corresponding notes.

At the town of Lyons, a tower seeming strangely out of place caught their eye. Seth pulled over once more and reached for his camera. Kayla craned her neck to see the top which stretched tall and stately above the surrounding trees. Flags flew from the corner turrets.

"I think we've stumbled into a time warp. This is surely medieval England," said Seth with a grin.

Kayla asked, "What in the world is it?"

"I've read something about this place. Unless I'm mistaken, there's a Frank Lloyd Wright connection," Jessica answered, referring to the famous architect.

"Let's see what we can find out." Seth checked for traffic in both directions, but before he could turn the motor home around, Jessica protested.

"We really should keep going if we're to make Joliet on time. They're expecting us at the Rialto at ten-thirty. I'd hate to keep them waiting."

Disappointment apparent, Seth flashed Kayla a conciliatory smile and murmured, "Remind me, and we'll catch it on the way back."

Kayla nodded and settled back again. The old road played out a few miles farther on, necessitating a brief stint on I-55. After a swift eight miles, they picked up the old route again.

Thinking of May back at the Jackson Street breakfast spot, Kayla commented, "The interstate may not have much personality, but the waitress is right. It gets you there in short order."

Seth caught her eye in the rearview mirror. Grinning, he accused, "Traitor! It's generic with a capital *G*."

Jessica took Kayla's part, asking, "What's wrong with generic? I, for one, don't like surprises when I'm traveling."

Seth wagged his head, arguing good naturedly,

"But there's nothing to see from the interstate. It bypasses America."

"Give me planes and trains and mass transit— whatever gets me there the fastest and the safest," said Jessica. She relented then, adding, "Though, judging by the growing interest in the old two lane highways, there're a lot of people like you, Seth. People who'd like to turn back the clock."

"It isn't an escapism thing," Seth defended. "Even the most ardent highway fans are quick to remember 66 was also a killer. Nicknames like 'Death Curve' and 'Bloody 66' compel you to remember the loss of life."

Kayla wished she had something to contribute to the conversation, if nothing more than to keep her mind occupied. But she knew very little about the old highway and even less about travel in general. As the conversation in the front seat grew into a lively debate of ideas, her thoughts drifted unwillingly to Richard. The certified letter, the photo of the woman, the man who'd come to the post office, asking directions to his house. One thing right on the heels of another.

She could not shake the eerie realization that she'd dated a man for months, thinking she knew him when she really did not. She'd prayed, asking God's help in dealing with the sting of betrayal. But it hadn't lessened a bit since first setting eyes on the photo hidden now in the folds of the envelope on which she'd taken notes in the restaurant. Who was this other woman in his life? And why?

Why, if there was someone else, had he continued to see her?

Kayla mulled that over as they wheeled on to Joliet and stopped for their tour of the Rialto theatre. The theatre, like the highway, had just recently celebrated it's sixty-sixth anniversary. Seth snapped quite a few shots, for it was a magnificent place, breathtakingly opulent with it's soaring marble walls and grand staircases and fabulous crystal chandelier. Only slightly less impressive was the energy and enthusiasm Jessica, who by her own admission was not a genuine fan of the old highway, injected into the taping.

Much of the tour and the interview, Seth told Kayla as they stood looking on, would end up on the cutting room floor. But Jessica, by her thorough research and carefully thought-out questions, was insuring a first-rate travel feature. Her meticulous method of pursuing the story differed from Seth's more relaxed approach, but she was getting the job done.

They tooled on, cruising America's Main Street through an assortment of small towns interspersed along fertile Illinois prairie. Seth pulled over now and again to take pictures of the landscape: rich, black farmland resting beneath a blanket of melting snow; a grain elevator dominating the silhouette of a rural village against the winter sky; a barn, lettered to advertise Meramec Caverns, a Missouri attraction close enough to the highway to be considered a Route 66 connection.

Kayla scribbled more notes at a truck stop where different alignments of the highway had, over the years passed first the establishment's front and then its back door.

They lunched in Lexington, a small town with a big heart for Route 66. The Illinois Route 66 Association held their annual reunion in Lexington with a two-day fair. According to the girl at the lunch counter, it was a gala affair, drawing thousands for the food, the crafts, the flea market, the antique car parade, and a host of other events.

Kayla saw Jessica point at her watch as Seth chatted with the girl. Seth drew the conversation to a close and the drive continued with several stops remaining and a lot of road to travel before calling it a night in St. Louis.

Sixty-odd miles further south, they stopped at a truck stop in McLean. Kayla jotted down that the Dixie Truckers Home, possibly the most famous truck stop in the country, had been catering to truckers since 1928 and was now home to the Route 66 Museum. She browsed the museum showcases, the travel store, and gift shop, then joined the others for a piece of pie. Jessica was still watching the clock. But Kayla, Seth, and Mark exchanged smiles as graying knights diagnosed the ills of politics, education, and today's youth at a rowdy, round-table discussion.

Atlanta, Lawndale, Lincoln, and a host of other Illinois towns blurred together as they motored steadily south and west. Ninety percent of the highway still survived in Illinois. And, by the time darkness fell, Seth's list of places he'd like to check out on the return trip had grown lengthy.

By dinner time, only one stop remained between them and their evening destination. It was not on Jessica's itinerary, so in her view, it was an unnecessary stop. But Seth held firm. He swung by an old gas station in one of the little towns, a station born the same year as the road. But the lights were out. The owners had gone home.

Not easily deterred, Seth parked alongside another motor home in a lot skirting a nearby café. Kayla stayed in the motor home with a fidgeting Jessica. She watched through the front window as the teenager running the place wagged her head and shrugged.

"Dead end," said Jessica, sounding relieved. She checked her watch and sighed. "I'm ready for a hot bath, a good dinner, and a warm bed."

"It has been a long day," murmured Kayla, sorry for Seth that his one detour from Jessica's rigid schedule had not panned out.

Another glance revealed Seth chatting with an older fellow at the counter. She saw him smile, then throw back his head and laugh. As the minutes ticked past, one gusty sigh and then another accompanied Jessica's restlessness. Finally, she moved toward the door.

"I'm sure Mark's eager to call it a day, too. I'll ride the rest of the way with him. Tell Seth we'll meet him at the Chain of Rocks bridge tomorrow morning at nine o'clock. Mark's going to tape him giving the history of the bridge. Different voices, different faces'll give the piece a nice mixture."

Kayla nodded agreement and went inside to join Seth. Upon learning Mark and Jessica had gone on ahead, he grinned and said, "Shook off the shackles, did you? Good! We can do our own thing." Indicating the gentleman at the counter, he introduced her, saying, "Kayla, this is Lowell Bridges. He and his wife are traveling the old route, just like us."

The old gentleman's mouth wrinkled into a grin. "Pleased to meetcha." With a bob of his head, he excused himself, saying, "I'm gonna go fetch my wife. Don't run off, now. I'll be right back."

Kayla watched him out the door, then asked in a low voice, "Who is he?"

"A man with a story." At her puzzled look, Seth draped an arm over her shoulder and chuckled. "That's what the old road is all about. The common man and his story."

seven

It was more than a story. It was an epic novel. Yet, as Lowell Bridges and his sweet-natured wife, Anna, shared a meal with Seth and Kayla in the small diner, it was the most fun Kayla had had all day. It wasn't just the stories. It was the Bridges, two people who'd traveled life together without growing weary of the company. Their gentle humor and tenderness toward one another was as natural as the ease with which Lowell finished Anna's sentences.

"Remember that Christmas back in Tulsa when a sleet storm kept our company from coming? I'd been cooking for days, and we had all that food," began Anna. Then she paused and smiled in anticipation. Just like she'd punched a button and was waiting for the favored record to drop. Lowell would pick up the story.

There were a lot of buttons, enough to last through a chicken dinner plus dessert. Lowell Bridges had lived a stretch of years, most of them along the old highway. As a boy, he'd carried water to the work crews building the road through his hometown in Oklahoma. He remembered the Bunion Derby and the foot-sore runners making their way through town in 1927, a publicity stunt acted out along the old road.

During prohibition, he'd hauled a truck load of fresh vegetables for a man he met in a restaurant only to realize, when the delivery address turned out to be a speak-easy, that he was delivering more than just okra and tomatoes! He'd pumped gas to Okies on the road of broken dreams. He'd hung out at a dance hall along the road while stationed at a base in Missouri. Bands, some of which came to be famous in later years, played and he danced with a lot of girls, Anna among them. And it was Anna he chose as a partner for life.

After the war, he got a job driving a charter bus up and down that old road. He'd seen the country's prettiest scenery, got caught in the most awful traffic snarls, witnessed more than a few fiery crashes, met a lot of nice folks and some not-so-nice ones, too.

At ten o'clock, the yawning waitress took off her apron, shut out some lights, and flung them a pointed glance. Seth picked up the tab, bought a pocket full of peppermints, and shared them as they walked out to their motor home and said goodbye to the Bridges.

As they motored on their way, a lonesomeness stole over Kayla. She'd have traded her job, her shop, and a good deal more for a soul mate such as the Bridges had found in one another.

Seth glanced her way as the headlights picked out the road in the darkness. "Penny for your thoughts."

"I was just relishing their oneness. Envying it some. And thinking it all too rare," admitted Kayla.

"Now, now. Don't get pessimistic on me," Seth said as a droplet of rain hit the windshield. "Josh and Shelly have a pretty good thing going. Stevie and Evan. And a few others I could name."

"Stevie and Evan?" Kayla echoed.

"Old friends," he said briefly.

"There's so many who lose it, though. It must break God's heart. It's scary."

"You? Scared? Since when?"

"Since I realized I don't know half as much as I thought I did. And that I'm a lousy judge of character."

"Now wait just a second," Seth chided. He slanted her a grin. "That hit a little close to home."

"I didn't mean. . .though now that I think of it . . . ." Kayla stopped, then began again, hesitantly picking her way along. "I'm not sure, even back then, that I knew you all that well. I ignored what I didn't want to see—that we were just too different. I thought I'd grown up since then. Learned my lesson. But here I am, falling right back into the same pattern."

Kayla lapsed into silence, thoughts so strongly on Richard, she failed to see Seth's reaction. Without warning, he pulled off on the shoulder. She blinked at the sudden brightness as the light came on.

"What's the matter? Why are we stopping?"

Seth swung around in the seat to face her. "What's

the lesson you haven't learned? The pattern you fear repeating?"

His tone alerted Kayla to her error. She wagged her head, color rising. "I didn't mean *us*. Not us *now*, anyway. Us, seven years ago, and now, Richard." Struggling to explain, she hung her head and admitted, "I found out yesterday that there's another woman in his life."

"I see. So you're blaming yourself, thinking you're a poor judge of character." A muscle rippled along the line of his jaw, as he searched her face.

Kayla ran her hand through her hair, uncomfortable with Seth's close scrutiny. "Look at my record. That's twice now I've struck out." Seth flinched. But his jaw remained set. Warily, he asked, "Is that why you came with me? To strike back at Richard? To hurt him like he's hurt you?"

There was nothing judgmental in his tone. Still, Kayla was quick to set him straight, claiming, "No, I just want to get away. I have to sort things out."

"What's to sort out? You find out a man you trust has been sneaking around behind your back, so of course you're hurt," Seth said. "And mad, I'd think."

Feeling the sting of unbidden tears, Kayla swallowed hard. "I guess I should be furious. But I'm not even sure what hurts. My pride, my heart. Mostly, I'm confused, bewildered." She swept a hand through her hair. "That sounds crazy, I know. It *is* crazy, the whole situation."

Seth was silent a moment. Searching her face, he said, "I'm probably not the one to bring it up, especially since I encouraged you to come on this trip. But it occurs to me that running away isn't the answer. You probably should have stayed and had it out with him."

Kayla slanted him a seeking look. "Is that what you would have done? Given my situation?"

"Sure. If you don't understand what happened, then how are you supposed to work through it?"

"Maybe you're right. Maybe I should go back," Kayla murmured.

"On second thought, there's no reason I should be robbed of your company," he said, slanting her a look that brought color to her cheeks. "Why don't you call him instead? The words might come easier over the phone."

He valued her company? Hardly seemed likely, as preoccupied as she'd been. Sweeping her hair back, Kayla grappled with the problem at hand. "A phone call is kind of awkward. Let me think about it," she said finally.

"If you want me to stop, let me know." Seth flicked off the light, put the motor home in gear, and guided it back onto the road. He tuned in some soft music and hit the wiper switch. The rain peppered down, re-beading the glass just as soon as it was slicked away.

Kayla's thoughts formed a similar arc, flitting from Seth to Richard and back again. There for a moment, Seth had thought she meant she'd fallen for him all over again. He'd thought *that* was the lesson she hadn't learned. An old familiar flutter stirred in her stomach. If she hadn't set him straight in such a hurry. . . .

Richard. Richard was the problem. Focus on the problem. To call him or not to call him. What was she to say? She could start by asking who it was he'd been seeing. Was it serious? And why had he played games instead of being honest with her?

She might just as well have shown Seth the picture. But for him to see Richard and that woman exchanging such an intimate smile—she'd feel like an even bigger fool. She didn't want Seth's pity. She never had liked anyone feeling sorry for her.

Was that why he'd invited her along on this trip? Because he knew the score where Richard was concerned and he hoped to cushion the blow a little? He had a good heart, Seth did. Success had not changed him, he was still tender-natured. Well-intentioned, even if his involvement did overstep the boundaries of casual friendship a bit. But then, that was just part and parcel of his take-charge nature.

And he was right—she ought to be furious with Richard. He'd betrayed her trust. She ought to ring him up, wring out a confession, and ring off! Except, she wasn't very good at that sort of thing. Peaceful by nature, she shrank from standing firm in confrontation, let alone initiating it.

"Though it's kind of late to be calling." Her

mental argument spilled into words.

"All the better for you. Catch him out of a sound sleep, and maybe you'll surprise the truth out of him." Seth sent her a sidelong glance and challenged softly, "Or could it be you're not quite ready for the truth? That you're shrinking from it?"

"Of course I want the truth!" she countered. "What makes you say that?"

Seth shrugged, thumbs absently tapping the wheel to the beat of the music. His lack of response raised her hackles. How like him to plant an idea like a needle and then just wait for her to back into it. Seven years wiser, she wasn't so quick to assume he knew what was best for her. Wasn't that how she'd lost herself in the first place—capitulating too easily, letting him do the thinking, the decision-making? Only when he was gone had she realized how devastating such total surrender had been to her self-confidence.

"I guess you're right," Seth offered out of the blue. "Face to face would be better. Unlike a phone call, Farrell can't hang up if he doesn't like the way the conversation's going."

Kayla shot him a narrow glance. Now, whatever route she took, the suggestion was his. She sucked the inside of her lip as they drove on through the dark, damp night. Fine lines framed his eyes, a smudge of fatigue beneath. No hint of clever manipulation.

What was the matter with her, anyway? Why had she become so suspicious, so defensive all of a sudden? Had Richard wrought this mistrust in her? Or was it that in the day spent together, her resistance to Seth had worn thin? She felt vulnerable. But the issue was not Seth and all that lay behind them. Richard's duplicity was the issue, and whether or not she wanted to come to terms with it. Seth's idea had been perfectly reasonable. There was nothing to be gained by rejecting it just because it was his.

She turned in the seat and said firmly, "Pull into the next town and find a phone, Seth. I'm calling."

Whatever his thoughts, he kept them to himself. A few miles farther on, the lights of a little town that had rolled up its streets hours ago glittered between sweeps of the wiper blades. Seth found a phone booth at the edge of a deserted service station. He stopped on the drive and left the motor running.

Kayla tucked her coin purse into her pocket, pulled her coat over her head, and scampered a few damp feet into the glass booth. She punched in the area code, followed by the familiar number. The operator requested ten cents more than she had.

"Can you hold on just a minute?" Kayla folded the door open and called to Seth in the motor home, "Could you help me out, Seth? I'm short a dime."

Seth cut the headlights and motor and stepped right into a puddle, splashing his shoes and the hem of his trousers. He squeezed into the booth, reached into his pocket, and held out a handful of change. "Enough?"

"More than." Kayla dropped in a dime, then backed against one wall.

Before Seth could get out, thunder cracked like a cannon. The skies dazzled brilliance and the heavens let loose with a downpour. It angled in the open door, rebounding as it hit into smaller showers that dampened her shoes and chilled her legs through her slacks.

"Close it before we both drown!" Kayla shivered and pulled her coat close as she made room for Seth. He backed against her the brief moment it took to fold the door closed, and she stiffened, resisting the warmth that spread like candle wax too close to the flame. It was hard to hear above the lash of the rain. She held a hand over one ear as the call rang through.

Seth was just inches away, shoulder resting against the glass wall. Raindrops glistened on his face and in his hair. The chill had erased the fatigue from his face. But he seemed edgy. He bent a knee, bracing the sole of his shoe against the wall. Drummed his fingers. Stretched the kinks from his shoulders.

"You'll want some privacy," he said finally and attempted to squeeze past her.

Kayla caught at his sleeve. "You can't go out there. It's pouring!"

"I won't melt."

"May as well wait it out, Seth. Richard's not home, anyway. It's just his machine," she said, as Richard's recorded voice came over the line.

"Wait a second." Seth stopped her from hanging up. "Why don't you leave a message?"

How did you capsulize all that needed saying into sentences brief enough to fit on a message machine? At a complete loss, Kayla tried again to hang up. Seth frustrated her attempt.

Faintly annoyed, she said, "I don't even know how to begin.

"Then allow me." Five o'clock shadow darkened the contours of his face as he held her wrist, the phone in suspension. A rakish smile trickled across, slow as molasses, not to be trusted. "With your permission, of course."

His fingers encircling her wrist made pulsing pressure points as he awaited her decision. Flustered, she freed her hand and cast caution to the wind. "What can it hurt? Be my guest."

"Farrell? This is Seth Brooks." Seth's deep voice filled the phone booth. "I'm cruising America's Main Street with your little treasure. Just called to say thanks."

eight

Leave it to him to be so free-wielding with *her* reputation! Kayla planted a hand on her hip. "Nice going, Seth. He's going to think I've thrown every last scruple out the window."

"Pretty good payback, don't you think?" Seth rocked back on his heels, looking pleased with himself.

Kayla swallowed a smile and rolled her eyes. "It's my fault. I should have known better. You're incorrigible, you know? Next time, I'll leave my own message, thanks all the same."

He shot her a languid grin. "If it's your good name your worried about, give it a rest. Folks who like you believe the best; those that don't believe the worst anyway."

Drily, she retorted, "Phone-booth philosophy. Get an 800 number, and you could go into business."

He smiled. "I've got all the business I can handle at the moment, trying to sooth your misery."

"I didn't say I was miserable!"

"Nope. You've been a good sport all day. But every now and then, I catch you looking like someone just ran over your cat." Seth touched her lips to still the rising objection. Mouth losing its

97

upward curve, eyes searching hers, he said quietly, "You don't have to pretend with me, you know. If you want to have a good cry, I've got just the shoulder."

He'd lost his bantering tone. His face was so tender, her pulse quickened. She swept her hair back and lifted her chin, saying, "I'll keep my tears. He isn't worth it."

Seth's eyes darkened. He captured her chin, his intentions clear enough to send her heart reeling. Yet he hesitated, watching her face. "You're sure?"

"About Richard?" She nodded, melting at his touch.

"That's good." The pressure of his thumb slackened. A finger caressed the delicate line of her jaw. Leisurely. Savoring. Spreading gooseflesh.

His gaze entangled with hers, measuring what lay between them. She saw her own yearnings mirrored in the blue of his eyes. Felt that tingling, tantalizing tug, simple and ageless as time.

"It feels good to touch you," his voice rumbled like distant thunder.

Her skin sizzled, lightning-stricken. "I don't think. . . ."

"Then don't," he stopped her, thick-voiced. "Just this once, don't think."

Terrible advice. She lifted a hand, then let it fall. He took it for acquiescence and framed her face between his hands, rubbing out a rain drop with the stroke of a thumb. Achingly tender. His fingers spread a shower of sparks, trailing through her hair and down her shoulders until the distance shrank and he gathered her in, saying softly, "Come here, you."

She trembled in his arms, his persistence spreading heat that defied the chill and the rain. Delicious sensations licked along nerve endings like sparks in a dry field, spreading wild fire. Red lights flashed in her heart, in her head. Kayla closed them out. Her arms stole around him as if of their own volition.

Seth buried his face in her hair. A sound rose from his throat, a low, wordless vibrato that swelled along her nerve endings. She lifted her face as his head came down. Met his lips and caught her breath. He tasted of rain and peppermint and old associations. Seven years melted away like a rain drop trailing down the glass. Her first love. Her only true love.

Tenderly he drew her closer, so close, his heartbeat melded with hers. "I've missed you. I've missed everything about you. Silken hair," his fingers sifted dark strands. "Green eyes, sweet laugh, sweet lips."

Lips that had declared love forever—a love that hadn't worked out. Kayla reached for resistance and found none. Not even a token. Never, in her wildest dreams, had she imagined Seth could penetrate defenses built expressly with him in mind. The rules that had governed her heart were ashes at his feet. He was thunder's boast and lightning's night fire. His kisses quenched her arid heart. She revelled in his strength, his masculinity, his aggression tendered by control. Richard was nothing. A cloud among clouds, easily lost. This, *this* was courting real heartbreak. This was madness.

"We're not thinking!" She caught a ragged breath. "We've been down this road before."

"We. . .should have. . .stayed on it," he whispered, mixing kisses with words.

A well-placed kiss sent chills down her spine. She lifted one shoulder, protecting her ear from further exploration and protested, "We were too young. Too different."

He kissed her fiercely and denied it, saying, "No, we were too willful, too ambitious, too careless with love. At least, I was."

She created space with her hands. Fingers spread across his chest, she widened that space. "Nothing's changed, Seth. Don't you see? We're still two very different people."

"Different is good. I like different. Me Tarzan, you Jane." He played the fool, trying to coax a smile, then chuckled at her straight-faced effort. "What a sad little face! Were you always this serious?"

"You're not listening," she said. "This isn't going to work. It didn't work before and it won't"

"Shh! You worry too much." He stroked the lines from her brow, his fingers a silent language, a potent argument.

Her heart was beating too fast, her thoughts battling emotions. She drew back another step, recognizing her own vulnerability. Wanting him, knowing better. A lightning rod reaching for the sky, attracting needless pain. She'd tasted brief joy, but reality worked like gravity. Her feet touched earth. "You're all-consuming, Seth. You take over everything you touch. I'm afraid—"

"Fear, that's the operative word." He rested a shoulder against the damp glass and dared to smile—as if he could coax her into forgetting that season of pain, that season of searching for a rock, a foundation after having been so totally adrift in him.

"I didn't even know who I was when you got through with me," she protested.

"Who said I was through?"

Face flaming, she sought desperately for words to make him understand her viewpoint. Clear words, without wounding. "You have a wonderful energy. A vividness that's blinding to the heart. You throw such a long shadow, Seth, you simply take over."

His expression shifted from surprise to protest. "That's twice you've said that. I don't recall taking over. I never meant to, anyway. There was always compromise between us."

To him, it probably seemed that way. Perhaps it was more her fault than his. She'd had too little confidence before to be open with him. To share her true feelings. She'd been bedazzled, in awe, so afraid of losing him, she'd tried very hard to be what she thought he wanted her to be. Compromising everything, even her faith. How was he to know how dearly it had cost her when she couldn't find the words to explain?

Inadequately, she said, "I'm not the same girl you left behind, Seth. God's changed me. I'm scared I can't be His woman and yours, too."

Her earnest explanation brought a ghost of a smile to Seth's lips. He reached out as if to touch her, then let his hand fall as she backed away. Softly, he murmured, "'Perfect love casts out fear.' Haven't you heard?"

"Only God loves perfectly," she protested, heart squeezing as she measured the whole situation with split-second recall. He'd said love words before, said them easily, held her with those words, then cut her loose. The yawning black hole of grief was too potent a memory. Mindful this time of treacherous ground, she whispered a soulful plea, "Backtracking's no good. Don't let's do this again."

"Do what? Love again? I never stopped. Never!" he said with quiet passion. "I look at you and the emotions are so fresh, it seems I've been away no more than a day."

"Seven years!" she cried. Her thoughts thinned from sluggish to lucid. Picking out past failures. Crowding. Reasoning. Casting up points to be made. "You've been everywhere. You've made a life for yourself so different from mine. Your friends are artists and writers and celebrities. I don't begin to know how to fit into that. You saw how it was today. I've got 'small town' written all over me. The Jessica Williamses of the world leave me tongue-tied."

To her surprise, he wagged his head and smiled. "It takes a lot less courage to know them than it does to know thieves and prostitutes and drug offenders and whoever else they've got locked up in the Kitterly County Jail."

She hadn't realized he was aware of her involvement in organizing a prison ministry. "It's not the same thing," she protested. "Knowing they need someone to listen, someone to care, someone to bring them to Christ gives me courage. I can't let you change that in me, don't you see? It's the best part of who I am."

"The Jessica Williamses of the world have the same need," he overlooked her reminder of the power he had, however unwittingly, once exercised in her life. "Beneath the skin, we're all the same. You know that."

His words ambushed her best argument. What had become of the agnostic? The cocky fellow who needed nothing and no one so much as to travel and write and make his own way? Afraid to trust what she was hearing, she stammered, "Are you saying we *do* have something in common?"

A muscle twitched along his stubbled jawline. In lieu of a reply, he folded the door and stepped out into the wet night. Hands outstretched, palms up, and his face lifted to the sky, he shouted above the pouring rain, "You know me, God. I'm not proud. I'll take her on the rebound. However I can get her."

So he *was* God's child, too! Tears filled Kayla's eyes. Sweet joy welled up inside. She was still a stay-at-home girl with her own quiet service to offer, and he, a road scholar with sights set on the next curve in the highway. But if in spirit their dwelling was in the shelter of the Most High, then maybe, they could find a home together.

Kayla joined him beneath their heavenly Father's cold, wet sky. "I'd like another chance, too. But let's not rush headlong, okay?" she cautioned. "Let's take our time. See if God's blessing is in it."

"Fair enough. I trust Him to decide." Seth's hand reached for hers.

She enfolded it between both of hers, then lifted her face to his. The stinging rain, as they kissed, washed away the pain and disappointment of the old road they had traveled and unfolded before them one bright and clean and shining with promise.

A short while later, as Kayla stepped out of her wet clothes and into a hot shower, the lines of a Psalm ran through her head. "I will say of the Lord, 'He is my refuge and my fortress, my God, in whom I trust. . . .If you make the Most High your dwelling, even the Lord, then no harm will befall you, no disaster will come near your tent.'"

It was a promise Kayla held close as she slid into her gown, hung her coat over a hot-air duct to dry, then peeked through the blinds of her hotel-room window. Out in the parking lot, the lights of Seth's motor home glowed. He too was preparing for a lonely bed. As the rain peppered down, thanksgiving poured from her heart. She prayed for guidance and for wisdom. The wisdom to distinguish God's plan for her future from her own heart's desire.

Kayla awoke early. She dressed in dark wool slacks and a warm geometric-print sweater that fell past her slim thighs. The green running through it matched her scarf and picked up the vividness of her eyes. She folded her nightgown into her suitcase, her still-damp sweater and slacks into a plastic bag, and let herself out just as the pale winter sun splashed a little color on the eastern horizon.

Dropping temperatures had turned last night's puddles to ice. Kayla skated cautiously across the lot and knocked on the motor-home door. Seth let her in.

"Morning," his greeting rumbled from a face freshly lathered in shaving cream.

Kayla smiled at bare feet protruding from the bottom of olive-green, straight-legged trousers and closed the door against the chill morning. "Looks like someone overslept."

He smiled from behind his creamy mask and dropped a kiss on her mouth. "Don't get smug with me, my little postmark. I was up two full hours before your light went on."

She made a face as the soapy taste of shaving cream burned her tongue. "Doing what?"

"Developing film. I figured with your organizational skills, you could correlate your notes with the pictures. A running journal will help a lot when I get into my book." He crossed to the sink and a mirror he'd banded to the cupboard door above it and picked up his razor. "With the bathroom doubling as a darkroom, things get a little cluttered. I can't get to the sink or the shower."

Curbing a smile, Kayla watched a moment as he twisted his mouth to one side and made a swath through the shaving cream. She picked up his camera, snapped a carelessly-focused shot, and quipped a caption: "A man and his razor."

He grinned and ordered, "Go kick the tires or something. You're distracting me."

"Am I?" She dimpled.

He shook his razor at her. "Next thing you know, I'll be bleeding. And you know how that goes over."

She grimaced, the very thought of blood making her lightheaded. Taking her hotel-room key from her pocketbook, she waved it in front of his face and suggested, "Why don't we trade space for a while?"

Seth tossed his toiletries into a leather kit, slipped into shoes and coat, and dashed across the parking lot, face still lathered in cream.

By the time he returned, clean-shaven and scented with the same musky fragrance he'd been wearing the first time they'd met, Kayla had bacon and eggs, orange juice, and hot coffee waiting. She wanted to build on the newly discovered foundation of faith they shared. Overcoming a shy hesitancy, she asked as they sat down at the cozy lunch nook, "Could we say grace together?"

Seth's hand closed over hers. Kayla bowed her head, one in spirit, as Seth praised God in simple phrases for blessings received. He asked for safe travel throughout the day. He mentioned Jessica and Mark, requesting harmony and a spirit of cooperation as they worked together. Kayla echoed his "Amen," and opened her eyes, relishing the day ahead.

Breakfast was a leisurely, lighthearted affair. Afterwards, she washed up the dishes while Seth gathered the pictures he'd developed. Kayla leafed through the photos as they motored down the old road toward their appointed meeting place with Jessica and Mark. She had the notebook on her lap and the envelope with her first notes.

Admiring the pictures, she said, "I guess I should number them on the back, then jot the numbers alongside the corresponding notes in the journal."

"That's pretty much what I had in mind," Seth agreed. "Read what you've got on that place we ate breakfast yesterday," he added, as she held up the picture of May.

Kayla pulled the envelope from the pile in her lap. As she began reading, the picture of Richard fell out. It landed on the floor near Seth's feet. He picked it up, glanced at it briefly, and passed it back without comment.

Kayla's color rose as she slipped it back into the

envelope. She started to read her notes aloud, then paused, feeling Seth's watchful gaze. He'd already seen the picture. Pride was a mute point. Still, it was difficult. She dropped her pen and swept her hair back from her face.

Voice brittle, she said, "If you're wondering about the picture, that's how I found out about the other woman in Richard's life."

Seth looked at her a long moment, his expression tender, yet guarded. At length, he admitted quietly, "I know, honey. Who do you think took the picture?"

nine

Stunned, Kayla's green eyes widened. A shadow clouded her happiness. "*You* took the picture?"

Seth nodded. "After a good deal of deliberation, I mailed it to Josh. He sent it to you."

"But how, where. . .?" She paused, thoughts refusing to fall into order.

"At the airport. The day I flew in to see the baby." Seth slowed to let a pickup truck get around him.

"But you didn't meet Richard until later that day, did you? Why would you take a picture of him?"

"It wasn't intentional. I was photographing a dignitary at the airport. I thought he might be someone important, and in my business, you never know when a picture of that sort might come in handy," Seth explained.

Beginning to understand, Kayla asked, "Then it was only by chance that you caught Richard?"

"That's right. I remembered him, though, later in the day, when he kissed you."

Kayla flushed and averted her face, uneasy all over again. As the sun shone warmly on the windshield, she took the photo out again and studied it closely. The woman had a mole at the left corner of her upper lip. She was young, tall, willowy, and blond. Stylish clothes and the glint of jewelry lent her a cosmopolitan bearing. A vague familiarity teased at her memory. But she couldn't quite bring it into focus. "Unless I'm mistaken, she flew into Milwaukee with Richard," said Seth.

"Why didn't you just tell me that Richard had another woman?" Kayla asked as she put the picture away.

"I didn't think you'd welcome my interference. Nor were my motives all that pure," Seth admitted. "I couldn't decide what to do. That's why I dropped the ball in Josh's court."

"I'd have thought *he* could have been honest with me. Or Shelly."

"I'm not sure Shelly ever saw the picture."

"But mailing it like that—"

"Try not to be too hard on us. I figured, and I suppose Josh did too, it'd be easier anonymously."

Easier for whom? Kayla wondered. A weariness settled over her.

Seeming not to notice her silence, Seth asked, "This woman, any idea who she is?"

Kayla wagged her head.

"Do you know a woman named Marion Stauffer?"

The name stirred Kayla out of her reverie. "She's an archaeologist at the university. She was in charge of the dig out at the Indian burial sites. But if you're thinking that's her in the picture—"

"No, I know it's not her. But she *was* at the airport that day." Seth reached for his sunglasses. He shot Kayla a searching glance. "Is this awkward for you? Maybe you'd rather not hear this stuff about Richard."

It *was* awkward. But even more troubling was the way Seth had handled the whole thing, taking the initiative, uninvited. She wished he hadn't sent the picture to Josh. It was a marvel Josh had kept quiet. Shelly, too, for that matter. Despite Seth's doubts, Kayla was sure Josh must have told Shelly. They were sorry for her, no doubt. She squirmed at the thought.

"Kayla?"

Realizing she'd lost the thread of the conversation, Kayla glanced his way. "You were saying something about Professor Stauffer. Was she with Richard, too?"

Seth nodded. "Moments after I snapped that photo, Richard kissed the blond, tucked her into a cab, and waved her away. A couple minutes went by, and Professor Stauffer pulled up in an old station wagon. Richard climbed in and kissed her too. No real passion, though. Looked more like a token kiss."

"Richard *kissed* Marion Stauffer? I wouldn't have figured her for his type at all! Though it's beginning to sound as if everyone is Richard's .... Oh, never mind!" Kayla stopped short, flushed with humiliation. "How is it you recognized Professor Stauffer?"

"I didn't. I described her to Josh and he recognized her," Seth explained. "He'd talked with the professor several times last summer when the theft of those Indian artifacts was discovered."

"You aren't saying Joshua thinks Richard's somehow connected with the thefts at the burial grounds, are you?"

"He's looking into it," Seth admitted. "We had a long conversation Friday while I was waiting for you to get off work. That's when I told him about the little scene between Richard and Marion Stauffer. That's not all. Sometime last week, the Internal Revenue Service got in touch with the department concerning Richard," he elaborated.

Richard's odd request concerning the certified letter came to mind. Kayla mentioned it to Seth, giving Richard's explanation. "He said the IRS was harassing him for money he didn't owe."

Seth frowned, trying to piece the puzzle together. "What do you suppose he hoped to accomplish by destroying evidence that he'd received the letter?"

"He claimed he was trying to hold them off a while longer—buy some time while he got together with his bookkeeper and went over his tax records."

"But what good would it do him to refuse their letter, when they were already in town, questioning him?"

"I don't know. He didn't mention them paying him a call," said Kayla. "Obviously, though, his tax troubles are serious, or the IRS wouldn't have notified the local police for cooperative help."

She had, during her short stint with the department, witnessed similar cases. They were very persistent, the IRS. But to suggest that Richard was involved in the thefts at the Indian burial site—that was quite a leap.

As if sensing her mixed feelings, Seth said, "As far as the artifacts go, Josh hasn't found any evidence that Richard's involved. He's simply checking it out to be thorough." Seth smiled and changed the subject, asking, "Where were we? Oh, yes. You were about to read back yesterday's notes."

Kayla let it drop. She read her notes off the back of the envelope, then copied them into the journal with the numbers of the corresponding pictures. But she found it hard to concentrate. It was wasted energy, wishing Seth had been straightforward with her from the beginning regarding the picture, especially when there were so many unanswered questions concerning Richard. What kind of guy had she been dating, anyway?

After a while, Seth stopped at a gas station and asked for directions to the Chain of Rocks Bridge. The attendant's directions led them down an old road shrouded by trees bent on reclaiming the land. The attendant had told them they'd have to walk the rest of the way to the bridge. While the bridge wasn't in sight, the interstate highway was. It snaked atop an embankment a short distance away. But despite the echo of busy traffic passing close by, the spot seemed secluded, as if upon losing it's usefulness, the world had sliced it off and cast it aside.

Jessica and Mark had already arrived. Seth pulled

off the side of the old road and parked the motor home behind the station's van. Jessica, dressed once again in black, climbed out and exchanged greetings with them.

"We'll have to crawl through the hole in the fence here and follow this dirt path," said Jessica. "Mark's gone ahead with the equipment."

"Ladies first." Seth held a piece of the chain link fence back to widen the opening.

Kayla followed Jessica, making an effort as she did to chat companionably. The sun was melting the frost from trees and the winter-bleached undergrowth flanking the narrow path. There was a purple hue to the tangle of limbs overhead as the buds swelled in advent of spring. A choir of birds warbled morning verses as the frosty grass crunched beneath Kayla's feet.

Her thoughts on the shoot ahead, Jessica looked around and wrinkled her nose. "So much for past grandeur," she said.

Looking past nature's splendor, Kayla noticed evidence of vandals. Cans, bottles, and other trash lay in the underbrush. Initials had been carved into the trunks of trees. Several hypodermic needles, even a spent shell, lay cast to the side of the path. Kayla shivered and stopped short as a thorny branch caught at her coat. She fell behind, trying to untangle herself without tearing the fabric.

"You coming?"

Freeing her coat, Kayla quickened her steps and caught up with Seth. Sensitive to locales, she was grateful for the hand he extended. The place made her uneasy. It wasn't just the trash and neglect. She felt instinctively wary.

"There it is!" said Seth.

The path widened to reveal the old bridge jutting out across the frigid waters of the Mississippi. It rose from the forested shore and stretched westward, making a turn way off in the distance. Kayla tried to shake off sinister feelings as Seth reeled off history concerning the bridge.

"They logged some horrendous traffic jams on this bridge," he said as he led her to the gate that closed it off. "See the turn there? The river current was such that they built the angle in the bridge to keep barges below from plowing in the pilings. That angle caused all sorts of problems for semi-trailers. And the building down there? It's an old pumping station." He squeezed her hand and smiled. "Picturesque old relic, isn't it?"

Kayla nodded, for there was a graceful aging quality that begged to be painted. The wind whistled through the iron girders. Encroaching tree limbs whined and scraped against the bridge near the shoreline. Ghost traffic. She shivered involuntarily and murmured, "Haunting, though."

Seth gazed across the bridge and nodded. "I guess so, in a way."

Trespassers had pried an opening in the gate. Thinking the shot would be more effective from the bridge, Jessica led the men through. Kayla turned her back to the wind. She stood on shore, hugging herself to keep warm, as Mark taped Seth giving a brief history of the busy thoroughfare that had once been the gateway to the west for everyone from the military to vacationers to freight-haulers.

Kayla was relieved when the shoot was over. They piled into their vehicles and left the isolated bridge behind to head into St. Louis. Landmarks were plentiful in and around the city: an art deco motel rumored to have sheltered mobsters in its hey day, a couple landmark fast-food joints, and a frozen custard stand among them.

It was late morning by the time they completed their St. Louis tapings. A lot of miles remained between them and their next scheduled stop. As Kayla had come to expect, Jessica wanted to get there post-haste. Having learned from yesterday's experience, Seth tactfully suggested that Jessica and Mark take off in the van.

"We'll meet you there in plenty of time," he promised.

As Kayla motored alongside Seth down the old highway now flanked by pale bluffs and beautiful forested hills, she found herself thinking once more of Richard.

Turning it over in her mind, she said, "You know, a fellow came into the post office Friday, asking where Richard lived. He claimed he was from the IRS."

Seth glanced away from the road, a frown pleating his brow. "Odd he'd ask you, when he'd gotten all the information he needed from the police."

Kayla nodded. "To be frank, I didn't quite trust the guy. But before I could ask for some identification, things got out of hand."

She went on to explain about the little boy with the bloody nose and how, when the excitement had all passed, the man was gone. "The moment I was able, I checked my cash drawer. He just *looked* like a guy who might rob you."

Adjusting the mirror, Seth murmured, "He may have been exactly who he said he was, but it wouldn't hurt to mention it to Josh."

Kayla glanced at her watch. "I doubt he'll be home until this afternoon.

"Then let's stop for an early lunch. We'll call after we've eaten."

They ate in a small-town café on a yellow formica table flanked by garish red benches. But the service was prompt and friendly, and the chicken-fried steak dinner, delicious. Kayla made a trip to the ladies, room while Seth fed change to a pay phone. He was paying the bill when she came out, but he told her as they rolled back onto the highway that Josh's description of the agent from the IRS didn't fit that of the man who'd questioning Kayla in the post office.

"Who was he, then?" Kayla wondered aloud.

"Beats me. Josh said it didn't sound like anyone he'd seen, either. But if your instincts were correct, you've got to wonder what kind of folks Richard's fallen in with. Present company excluded," he added, slanting her a cautious glance.

Anyway Kayla looked at it, her association with Richard was an embarrassment. She wished as the miles sped past that he would fade from her life like the ribbon of highway behind them.

An hour down the road, Seth slowed the motor home and pointed out the tin roof of a faded red barn just beyond a broken-down fence.

"I perfected my free-throws in that old barn. Dreamed dreams of making the pros." He shot her a sheepish grin and added, "Never mind that the girl down the road could sink it from the other end of the barn. She had a better hook shot than me, too."

Kayla gave the leaning, vine-trailed barn a second glance. It was nestled between winter-brown hills. The tobacco ad on the roof had almost faded into oblivion. Nature seemed bent on reclaiming the little white house in the shadow of the barn, too. From their college days, she remembered that Seth had spoken occasionally of having spent much of his childhood in Missouri. "This is where you lived?"

He nodded. "The house has been vacant for years. Do you want to take a look?"

"Isn't that trespassing?"

"Only if someone objects," he said with a grin. "I don't think anyone will."

Pleased he should want to share this part of his past with her, Kayla poked around for the shoes she'd slipped off. "How old were you when you lived here?"

"Moved in about fifth grade and stayed until Josh and I had both graduated from high school." He slowed to a crawl, avoiding rain-filled ruts in the short lane.

What looked rustic from the road was, at hand's length, plain old neglect and decay. Windows were missing from the house. The porch sagged, and the front door was boarded up. A maple tree grew up out of a crumbling water reservoir. Even the railroad tracks just beyond it seemed to have fallen on hard times. Grass had grown between the rails, and the ties needing replacing. Seth climbed out and wandered toward the tracks, fingertips in his pockets.

"The railroad parallels much of Route 66," he said as Kayla fell in step with him. "Between trains blowing lonesome and truckers sounding their horns, it was enough to give a boy a good dose of the wanderlusts."

"Excuses, excuses," Kayla said softly. Noting the faraway look in his eyes, she slipped her hand into his to draw him back to the present.

He inclined his head, smiling. "Dad was on the road a lot, and Mom worked at a diner in town. That left Josh and me to our own devices. We hiked, biked, or chugged through the hills on a worn-out tractor. When Old Smokey wouldn't run anymore, we started jumping freights. We'd ride twenty miles to town and, in the afternoon, catch another one back."

"Your mother knew?"

"Not until Stevie told her. Then, believe me, she wore us out!"

Kayla smiled. "Stevie?"

"The neighbor girl. She was tomboy to the core, had the best set of arms around when it came to baling hay. You didn't want to mess with her, though. I learned that the hard way."

"When she told on you?"

"Yep. Pure revenge, it was. She'd jumped them herself. Plenty of times."

"You were sweet on her, weren't you!" Kayla guessed with a smile.

"Josh and his pals and I all had a crush on her," he said with a grin. "They were older than me, of course, and intuitive enough to doubt their affections would be welcomed. So they put me up to testing the waters."

"How?"

"Offered me a dollar if I'd tell Stevie she was pretty. I thought it over all the way to school and decided I could sweet talk her better than that."

Kayla smothered a chuckle. "Cocky even then, weren't you? What'd you say?"

His lashes came down, hooding twinkling blue eyes. "I sauntered right up to her, declared, 'You're lookin' hot today, Stevie,' and planted a big old kiss on her lips."

"My, my. You *were* cocky!"

He gave a short laugh, stroked his throat absently, and recounted, "She grabbed me with one hand, pinned me to a hot brick wall, and chocked me until

I hollered."

Kayla threw back her head and laughed.

Chagrinned, he drawled, "I wasn't long in taking it back."

"The compliment or the kiss?" asked Kayla, still laughing.

"Both. She cut school and went straight to my mother and told her every misdeed I'd ever done. Put me off girls for a long while."

"Yeah, yeah," said Kayla, knowing better.

Shared laughter took them to the yawning doors of the barn. Seth knocked down a wealth of cobwebs. He scouted out a rickety ladder leading into the loft and led the way up. It was dark and danksmelling. Kayla waited as he crossed the plank floor and flung open a wide door. He dusted a spot on the floor for her, then beckoned, saying, "Nice view. Come have a look."

They sat down side by side, legs dangling out the second-story door.

"Used to look a lot higher than this," Seth reflected wistfully. "Josh and I would pile up leaves and straw and hay and jump out. Stevie caught us at it once and laughed us into disgrace. Said her granny had more grit than us. Then she leaped out over the pile and landed on her feet."

Intrigued, Kayla said, "So where is this Stevie now? In Hollywood, doing stunts?"

"She grew up Hollywood material, all right. One very handsome woman," he said with enough of a sigh to stoke the fires of Kayla's imagination. "But

she married the art teacher the day after she graduated high school. If you think we're too different,
you should hear about them."

Kayla slid Seth a cautious glance, wondering if
this conversation—or even the unexpected stop—
was so innocent, after all. Suspicious, she asked,
"Does this story have a point?"

He shrugged. "I'll stop if I'm boring you."

"No, no," she said quickly. "Go on."

He drew his legs in and turned to rest his back
against the door frame, feet crossed at the ankles.
She leaned against the opposing frame, facing him.
A brisk spring breeze whisked through the open
door, toying with her hair. She held it out of her
eyes, watching his face as he continued.

"Evan Jones, that was the art teacher's name,
was fresh out of school and green as July corn. He
was slight and pale with a timid face and a high
voice that hardly rose above a whisper. We sized
him up the first day and gave him a week. Two, at
the outside."

"Poor man," she said, wagging her head.

"You get the picture. Everyone did. Except Stevie.
She fell for him hard. Circulated the word that
anyone who messed with him, messed with her."

"Did anyone?"

"Not after the first week—see, the boys couldn't
fight her. The ones who didn't worry about appearances worried about getting whipped. It was im-
possible in these hills to live down getting whipped
by a girl."

Kayla laughed. "So Stevie had them all over a barrel. I think I like her. Does this story have a happy ending?"

"They're still married, if that's what you mean. Still complimenting one another's differences. Would you like to meet them?"

"This story *does* have a point!" she accused and he grinned.

"Sure it does. So do you or not?"

"Makes no difference to me." She got to her feet and dusted off the seat of her pants, trying hard to conceal her curiosity.

"I'm a busy man. Make up your mind," he chided, blue eyes smiling as he rose beside her.

"I'm going down," she said.

"Let's jump. For old times sake," he coaxed, catching her hand.

She laughed, finding his playful side as appealing as ever. Richard, in retrospect, seemed hopelessly stuffy. "You jump first, then maybe I'll try."

"Together," he urged, hand gripping hers. "Seth and Kayla, taking the plunge, metaphorically speaking."

"Dangerous, if you ask me." She dragged her heels, offering a token protest as he pulled her toward the door.

"It's not that far. And there's leaves. Look!"

"Cold, wet, soggy leaves," she protested.

"Just jump, you big sissy. My granny's got more grit than you," he taunted, grinning.

"Oh, yeah?" She measured the distance, took a

deep breath, and jumped, pulling him out with her.

They hit the ground rolling, a tangle of limbs and wet leaves and laughter. He took advantage, just like she'd known he would, and wouldn't let go when she tried to get her feet under her.

"Not so fast. Where you think you're going?" he asked, nuzzling his way up her neck.

"Busy man. Real busy," she mocked him lightly.

"Shut up and kiss me. We're working on a relationship here, remember?"

"This isn't the part that needs work," she said with a giggle.

But he kissed her anyway. Kissed her so thoroughly, she stopped protesting and savored the fireworks until the cold wet ground crept through her clothes. Reluctantly, she put some daylight between them. Lips tingling, she picked a leaf out of his hair. "We'd better get going before Jessica sends out a search party."

"We've got a little time yet."

It was the inflection in his voice as he reached for her again that hung, an unspoken suggestion. She left it there, and got to her feet, a deep blush the only indication she followed his train of thought. Twelve days ahead of them yet. She'd thought she was strong in the face of temptation. But this wasn't going to be easy.

"Sorry," he said, not quite looking at her as they started back.

"It's okay," she murmured, uncomfortable now.

"Guess we'd better stay out of haymows."

Out of each other's arms, rather. It was a damp, chill forty degrees out, and she was burning inside.

"Want to talk about it?" he asked.

"No."

"Why not? We're not kids. We can talk about it."

"Maybe later," she said, for he was right. They were going to have to talk about it. Pray about it. Purity was an issue, a very big issue, especially alone in close quarters loving him the way she did.

ten

Seth regretted his lapse. Wanted to point out, if she'd only talk about it, that he'd come to it late, this business of making God Master of everything—including desire. Was that a lame defense, to claim he was still learning? Lame, maybe. But the truth. He'd like to explain, too, that he wanted her forever, and that he hadn't apologized for feelings both natural and healthy. He'd apologized for tempting her to yield.

What was it she'd said—she was afraid she couldn't be God's woman and his woman, too? Nothing like proving her point! He could reassure her, though—if she'd only let him—that the desire between them was in God's safe-keeping. Seth wouldn't tempt her again. Not until their union could be an honorable one. Which might take a while, judging by her concern over whether or not God seriously intended two people with their differences to become one.

He'd tried to tell her about Stevie and Evan. Evan, city-born and reared, frail and artistic. Stevie, herder of cows, tiller of soil, tough and earthy and uncompromising as the Missouri bluffs. Only a God of endless possibilities would draw those two together! One with a sense of humor, at that. He and Kayla, by comparison, seemed custom-designed for each other.

He slowed for the gate and winged Kayla a glance, saying casually, "Evan and Stevie's place has a Route 66 connection that reaches back a couple generations. Stevie's grandparents and then her daddy raised fruit and vegetables and sold them to those passing by."

"They still run a market?" Kayla asked.

He wagged his head. "They moved this old school house in here a few years ago as a shop for Evan. He does pricey oil paintings and some decorative gourds that move really well. Stevie has her hands full growing the things and drying them out for him to paint."

"Sounds interesting," mused Kayla, shrugging into the coat she'd just discarded.

Seth guided the cumbersome motor home over the cattle guard and through the gate. There were no other vehicles in the lot, and the shop, with it's spattering of paintings splashed across vivid white walls, was empty.

"Anybody here?" he called as Kayla wandered toward a display of painted gourds.

"Go away," a disembodied voice called back.

He grinned and retorted, "How'd you know it was me?"

There was a pause. "Seth?"

He faltered, for the voice, though feminine, sounded too thin, too reedy for Stevie's. Seeing Kayla's eyebrows jerk to attention, Seth strode toward the workroom at the back of the shop. It'd been a cloak room at one time. There were no windows, and the light was out. Stevie sat at the table, work-toughened hands curled around an empty coffee cup. Her flannel shirt was misbuttoned, and her hair was uncombed. An uneasy feeling washed over him.

"Stevie? What's the matter?"

"What isn't?" she countered and sighed deeply.

"You sick?"

"No." She swept a hand through tousled hair and lifted dark-shadowed eyes to his face. "What're you doing here, anyway?"

"I brought a friend along. Someone I'd like you to meet. Why are you sitting in the dark?"

"Just sitting. Thinking," she said, her voice subdued. She raised a listless hand. "Give me a moment to tidy up and I'll come meet your friend, okay?"

"Sure." Mystified over the change in her, Seth started away, then turned back. "Look, if we've caught you at a bad time, we can stop in another time."

"Is this friend a 'she' friend?" Stevie asked.

He nodded.

"Then I'd better warn her about you, hadn't I?" she asked, sounding more like herself.

Relieved, he chuckled. "Don't get too gussied up. I don't want to make her jealous."

She snorted. "Men. What do we get mixed up with you for in the first place?"

To his amazement, she burst into tears. He paused in the doorway, too stunned to retreat, too numb to be tactful. "You and Evan have a fight?" he blurted out.

She shook her head, her tangled mane of hair hiding her face.

"Where is he, anyway?"

"Gone."

"Gone where?"

"Arizona."

"What for?"

"It's too damp here."

"You mean, he's not coming back?"

A low sad moan and "It's not that simple" was all the answer he got. Having no idea how to help Stevie, he crept back out to the showroom. Kayla was all eyes.

"Did we come at a bad time?" she whispered.

"Apparently so." In a few soft-spoken words, he relayed what'd happened.

"Maybe they just had a spat," she suggested.

"I don't think so." Some object lesson! What an irony! He thrust his hands in his pockets and murmured, "Maybe we'd better go."

"Go? We can't leave her like this."

"What can we do?"

Kayla hesitated a long moment, her face a study of compassion. "I don't know. Listen, maybe?"

He wished they were fifty miles down the road at their next shoot. He wasn't good at this tears thing.

"Seems you're the closest thing she's got to a friend at the moment," Kayla prompted gently. Hearing footsteps, he swung around. Stevie, still tall and stately and a little imposing, emerged from the cloak room. She'd washed a skin prematurely wrinkled by the sun. Her misbuttoned shirt was tucked into her trousers, and her long, straw-colored hair was tied back with a scarf. Her red-rimmed eyes were dry, but a haunting sadness lingered there as she stepped forward and offered a brown hand to Kayla.

"So your Seth's friend. Nice to meet you."

"Kayla Colter. Kayla, this is Stevie Jones," Seth introduced them.

"Stephanie," she corrected, turning dark eyes on him. "You and a few old-timers are the only ones who still fall back on that old nickname."

Seth smiled and said easily, "You'll always be Stevie to me. Stevie, the Amazon."

She laughed a shadow of her real laugh and cautioned Kayla, "Better watch this one. He's slick."

Seth grinned. Careful not to mention Evan, he told Stevie why they'd come. "I'm working on a Route 66 project. Thought your family would fit in nicely—your connection with the highway going back the way it does."

It was an easy topic for Stevie. She invited them to sit down and, over coffee, recounted half-a-dozen road stories. Stories that smoothed over hard times and hard work and even heartbreak with a matter-of-factness that was poignant. But it wasn't until they were leaving that Stevie shook Seth's hand and murmured, "I'm sorry about that little cloudburst back in the cloak room. I'm selling the place, in case you hadn't heard."

"Selling! You're kidding!"

"Evan's got a lung ailment. Doctor says a drier climate is about the only thing that's going to help him. He's out there now, trying to find us a place."

"That's rough, Stevie. I know how you love this old place."

Her sad eyes filled, but she blinked them dry. "There's a lot of good memories here."

"Just like with the road," said Seth, and she nodded.

"It hurts. I won't say it doesn't. But you do what you have to do." She thrust a hand toward Kayla and said with a bittersweet smile, "Take care of this boy. He's only aggravating most of the time."

Seth watched Kayla smile. He felt a glow of pride in her tenderness as she reached past Stevie's hand for a quick hug.

"I'm glad I got to meet you. I'll be praying God makes Evan well again."

Color rose to Stevie's cheeks, but she lifted her chin and countered, "That's a good prayer. Thank you. Means a lot, you two stopping by."

"Keep in touch, Stevie. We want to know how things come out," Seth said, as she walked them out, and she nodded agreement.

"Courageous woman," mused Kayla, once they were underway again. Noble, too. True to her covenant when times turned tough.

"It's going to be rough for her," murmured Seth.

Kayla nodded, a prayer in her heart.

Short of time now, Seth cheated and took the next on-ramp to the interstate. Route 66 was still there, a scrawl weaving between big-shouldered bluffs.

Kayla watched it wind onward, her thoughts on Seth's old friend. It *was* going to be rough. But God honored covenant keepers.

As if sensing her thoughts, Seth reached across the console and squeezed her hand. "Stevie'll be all right. She's enduring, just like the old road."

They were twenty minutes late for the next stop on the itinerary. Jessica was edgy over the wait, but she conducted herself like the professional she was and the remaining shoots came off smoothly.

As soon as their work was done, Jessica went over the next day's schedule, then motored off toward the interstate with her camera man. So it was that dusk found Seth and Kayla in a town consisting of a string of houses and businesses interspersed along both sides of the old highway.

"Looks like your kind of place," said Kayla with a smile.

Seth slowed to a crawl and pointed out an antique shop on the outskirts of town. Flanked by woodlands to the north and the west, it had the look of a nineteenth-century general store. The shop owner, nearly as dated as the false-fronted building, stepped outside on the boardwalk.

Kayla lowered the window and called, "Are you closing?"

"Not if you're coming in," the old woman called back.

Kayla questioned Seth with a glance. He nodded agreement and parked the motor home in the adjoining lot.

Cowbells, strung to the door by a leather strap, jingled as Seth and Kayla walked in. The elderly proprietress leaned on her broom and appraised them with a sharp-eyed glance. "Traveling, are you?"

Kayla smiled and nodded. "We won't take long, though, if you're wanting to close."

"Take all the time you need. Let me know if you have any questions." The woman resumed sweeping.

Everything about the shop reminded Kayla of a simpler time: the cameo brooch adorning the plain dark dress of the ruddy-cheeked shopkeeper, the gas light fixtures displayed overhead, the sawdust compound littering the floor.

Seth wandered away, his attention captured by a collection of old farm tools. Kayla admired a display of dolls. Some were authentic antiques, others, well-crafted reproductions. She picked out a Kewpie doll to take back for her namesake.

A large room to the rear of the store proved a treasure-trove of furniture. The familiarity of the craftsmanship excited Kayla. "Seth? Come look at this."

He ambled toward her, his gaze inquiring.

"These pieces are very much like some Richard stored in the depot. They were crafted in Philadelphia and sold in 1876 at a big fair held to commemorate America's centennial."

The proprietor, following on Seth's heel, spoke up. "I see you know a bit about antiques."

"Not nearly as much as I have yet to learn," Kayla confessed.

"Then perhaps you'd be interested in knowing that some pieces by the same furniture maker are on display in the Blair House in Washington, D. C."

Kayla nodded, for Richard had told her that as well. As twilight shadows turned the sheer white curtains lavender, she felt a twinge of sadness over his tax troubles and the suspicion cast upon him.

"Lie on your back and scoot under the bed there. Go ahead," urged their self-appointed guide. She framed a wrinkled smile and instructed, "Close your eyes and don't open them until I tell you."

Kayla exchanged glances with Seth. He grinned and shrugged. Faintly ill at ease, she got down on all fours.

"All right now, open your eyes," the woman ordered once Kayla was flat on her back beneath the bed.

Kayla gasped. "Come here, Seth. You've got to see this."

He squirmed beneath the bed to lie next to her. There was a mirror on the underneath side of the bed, throwing back their reflection. "What's the idea?"

"You lift the bed up so it stands against the wall," the woman said. "The mirror is displayed, giving it the look of a wardrobe."

Seth pulled a playful face in the glass. He planted his thumbs at his temples and waggled his fingers at Kayla, then smothered her giggle with an impromptu kiss. Heart beating fast, she laughed softly and whispered, "Quit now, before she chases us out of here with her broom."

"Folks in those days appreciated a bit of secrecy," the lady was saying as Kayla crawled out from beneath the bed all rosy-cheeked. Seth shoved his hands in his pockets, the picture of innocence.

Anticipating the revelation of her own secret, the shopkeeper revealed a hidey-hole concealed in a post at the foot of the bed. "A lady might want to stash her favorite bits of jewelry here."

The elderly woman went on to show them a cleverly concealed compartment in the chest of drawers. "It was no doubt used for deeds and wills and other important legal papers. And take a look at this combination desk-bookcase. Think of the time involved in the carving. What a labor of love!"

In no apparent hurry, the woman guided them from one extraordinary piece of furniture to another. Before leaving the shop, Kayla bought a hand-carved train for Brent and several trinkets to display at the grand opening of her own shop. At Seth's request, the shopkeeper mentioned a café several blocks back the way they'd come.

"I could use some fresh air. And the wind's died down. Let's just walk," Seth suggested. He took the keys from his pocket and locked the motor home. Hand in hand, they turned back up the road.

Kayla paused beneath a street lamp and brushed Seth's hair with her free hand. "You've picked up a cobweb."

"Nothing crawling in it, I hope."

"Too dark to see." She raked her fingers through his hair for good measure. "That ought to take care of any wildlife."

He laughed and slipped his arm around her waist as they resumed walking. "Remind me not to indulge you in more antique shopping. Crawling under beds is beneath the dignity of a photo-journalist of my stature."

Kayla's laughter mingled with his. "Yes, you certainly did have that dignified appeal—making faces in the glass."

"How appealing? Irresistibly so?" The playfulness cleared the air of the pensive mood lingering in wake of their visit with Stevie.

"Weren't you always?" Kayla said softly.

He chuckled and drew her closer to his side. "And you always were good company. Today's been nice. We've got the whole evening ahead of us. Maybe we should drive on into Springfield on this old lover's lane and find a fancy restaurant to celebrate."

Cherishing his closeness, his warmth, she smiled. "Celebrate what?"

"Getting back together."

"I thought we were still deciding about that," she responded carefully.

He sighed. "Never should have stopped at Stevie's."

"That has nothing to do with it."

He looked at her closely. "It's not Richard, surely. I just naturally assumed, when you said he wasn't worth your tears. . . ." He faded and started up again. "Maybe it's high time I ask. How *do* you feel about Richard?"

"I feel stupid about Richard. Stupid and naive and soon to be the laughing stock of Kitterly."

"Come here." Seth coaxed her close. He nuzzled her cold cheek with warm lips and said in a low voice,

"You're none of those things. You're so easy to love. I thank God Richard or some other fella didn't snap you up. Wanna get married?"

"Now you *are* getting ahead of yourself." Touched by his tenderness, yet uncertain of God's intentions for them, she slipped out of his arms and resumed walking.

"How about tomorrow, then?"

It felt good to laugh. Kayla took his hand and pulled him along to the diner. The food was mediocre, but the place had a lamp-lit ambience conducive to whispered confidences. They talked a long while, touching on their shared past, their shared faith, and finally on the desire that flared so quickly between them. Kayla was touched by Seth's protective manner, yet held him no more responsible than herself.

Could this work? God-willing, she wanted to share a home and children and a life with him. They lingered a while over dessert, then she excused herself to freshen her lipstick while Seth paid the bill.

The restrooms were down a narrow hall with a fire exit beyond. As Kayla came out, a man exited the men's room across the narrow alcove. Hat pulled low, wool scarf covering his mouth, he stepped back, politely motioning for her to precede him.

Kayla shrugged one arm into her coat as she started down the dim alcove. But the moment her back was turned, the man overpowered her. His hand closed over her mouth before she could scream. A nightmarish unreality consumed her.

His grip mashed her lips against her teeth and she

tasted blood. She wailed a muffled scream and lashed at him with one free arm, kicked mercilessly, but she was half his size and tangled up in her coat and her pocketbook strap. Kayla was no match, simply no match for his strength.

eleven

The man dragged Kayla out the fire exit. Gut-clutching crime scenes from her academy classes flashed before her eyes as the warmth and safety of the restaurant gave way to the cold dark night. Terror rose to choke her, but her screams were silenced by a cruel gloved hand. The man hauled her, kicking and fighting, down a steep incline.

Kayla broke free on a plank bridge that crossed a narrow creek, but he caught her just a few steps farther on and forced her uphill into a thick stand of timber. She couldn't die! Not now. Not when she had so much to live for.

My fortress, my refuge, my God in whom I trust. The words raced through Kayla's mind as the man dragged her up the hill, deeper into the woods. *My shelter, my shield, my protector!* Prayer held panic at bay. Kayla clung to her composure by a narrow thread.

Out of breath, her assailant finally stopped. He sucked in wind in grating gasps that matched her own. "I'm not going to hurt you. All I want is the loot."

Kayla's purse was trapped on her shoulder by her coat sleeve. She pawed through it with one trembling hand and flung down her wallet.

139

"Don't play stupid, lady! You know what I mean!"

She tried to shake her head and couldn't, imprisoned by his rough arms.

"I'm going to take my hand away. Scream, and you're dead," he warned in a guttural voice.

Nodding, Kayla feigned cooperation.

Slowly, the man lowered his hand, but he kept an arm hooked around her neck. The pressure of it threatened to choke the smallest sound.

Her throat burning, trying hard not to cry, Kayla stammered, "Who are...are you? Wh...what do you want?"

"Rattlesnake's on to your boyfriend. He wants the treasure."

"What boyfriend? What treasure?"

The arm tightened, bringing tears to her eyes. "I'm out of patience, lady. For the last time, what have you done with the loot?"

Fearing she'd pass out if the arm tightened again, Kayla managed a hoarse, "It's stashed back in Kitterly."

The arm loosened a fraction. "You better not be lying to me."

"It's...it's...." Thoughts racing, Kayla faked a sneeze, then tried to reach into her purse. "I need a tissue," she whimpered when the man's arm tightened.

"What've you got in there?" He jerked so hard at the purse, the strap broke, coming free of her shoulder. As he plunged his hand inside the purse, she brought up her knee, practicing a self-defense technique drilled into her during her police training. His curses rang after her as she tore off through the woods, running blindly.

The lights of town shone dimly through the trees to her left, giving Kayla her bearings. Hearing her assailant crashing through the trees after her, she fell into a fence, picked herself up and scrambled over. Her coat caught on the barbed wire. She slipped out of it, flung herself to the ground on the other side, and resumed running. Brambles tore at her clothes. The twigs of low-hanging branches stung her face, as out of the darkness, a dog lunged.

"Oh, dear God, no!" she sobbed.

Miraculously, the dog brushed past and kept running. His deep-throated barking faded as the distance between them grew. She was never to know for certain, but she felt in that moment that the vicious-sounding dog was preventing her attacker from coming over the fence after her. A miracle dog, God's answer to prayer.

Kayla raced down hill toward the lights of the village, tripped over a root, and rolled headlong into a tree. Head throbbing, she struggled up and ran on. The trees gave way to a narrow creek. She leaped across and broke through ice on the other side. The stinging cold penetrated her shoes as she fought through a tangle of weeds and tough grasses. A fence was all that stood between her and a dark parking lot. Crippled by pain in her side, she half climbed, half fell over the fence. Seth's motor home was the only vehicle left in the lot.

He must have heard her coming, for he charged around the motor home. The strain of concern turned to relief at the sight of her.

"Kayla! You weren't in the restroom. I came back here and you weren't here either, then I—" He stopped short at her hoarse cry.

She ran to him, clothes torn and soiled, twigs caught in her hair. He let out a startled cry and raced to meet her. Shivering and weeping aloud, she flung herself into his arms.

"Kayla! What happened? Are you hurt?" His heart slammed as violently as hers as she clung to him, gasping for breath, sobbing, trying to explain. He smoothed her hair with a trembling hand.

"Inside, before you freeze." Seth half led, half carried her to the motor home.

Fresh tremors ran through Kayla as Seth turned on the light. The motor home had been trashed! Stunned, she stopped short. "You were robbed!"

Seth gave a terse nod, his gaze frantic as he took in her disheveled appearance. He jerked a blanket off the bunk, wrapped it around her, and pulled her down on his lap.

"You were robbed!" she said again. "And I was mugged! Seth! What on earth. . .? Why would anyone. . .?"

"Are you hurt?" he cried again.

"I'm okay. Scared, but okay," she stammered, lungs aching from running, from fear.

"All right then. Take it easy," he said as much to himself as to her. "I called the police when I couldn't find you."

"There was a man waiting outside the restroom. He grabbed me and pulled me out to the woods. He said something about a treasure, about loot. He seemed to think. . . ."

Beginning to think past survival, Kayla leaped to her feet. "If the police hurry, maybe they can catch him."

The county sheriff arrived within minutes, but a search of the restaurant as well as the woods turned up only Kayla's purse and coat, nothing more. The next hour was a nightmare of questions and answers, resolving nothing.

When the police finished their work, Kayla showered and changed while Seth straightened up after the intruder. As Kayla came out of the bathroom, Seth wondered aloud if all that had happened could in any way be connected with Richard.

At first, Kayla dismissed the suggestion outright.

"Think it over," Seth insisted. "Suppose Farrell *did* steal those artifacts? Suppose it was this character Rattlesnake who came to the post office looking for Richard that day. Suppose he was after the artifacts."

"But why would he come after us?"

"Maybe Richard sent him." Seth's eyes flashed as he pieced together a grim scenario. "Maybe it was a diversion to throw the fellow off his trail."

"But Richard doesn't know—"

"Yes, he does. The message on his recorder!" All the color drained from Seth's face. "Kayla, I as good as drew him a map!"

Kayla's mouth went dry. It seemed such an unlikely set of circumstances. And yet, she *had* been attacked. And, though ransacked, the motor home hadn't been robbed. Seth's costly cameras, his laptop computer, even his traveler's checks left carelessly in plain view, were all passed over. So what was the intruder searching for, if not artifacts?

"Maybe," she said finally. "Should we go back to the police?"

"Not yet," said Seth. "Let's call Josh first."

Seth pulled out of the parking lot and stopped at the first pay phone. Nervous after all that had happened, Kayla watched from the motor home as Seth dialed, hung up, and dialed again. The conversation was brief, and when he returned, she could tell that the news was not good. But never, never for a moment did she dream his grim expression had nothing whatsoever to do with the mystery surrounding Richard.

"What is it? What have you learned?"

"They've taken the baby to the hospital."

"The baby?" cried Kayla, heart plummeting. "What's wrong with her?"

"I don't know. I called the sheriff's office when no one answered at home. All I know for sure is Josh and Shelly are at the hospital with the baby."

"I've got to get home. I've got to be there for Shelly. If anything happens to that little girl. . . ."

"Pray, honey. Just pray." Seth held Kayla tight for a moment, then eased her into the seat. "Springfield's not far. Maybe you can get a flight out tonight."

Kayla nodded, grateful for his quick thinking when

her own mind had gone numb. "What about you?"

"I can't leave without getting in touch with Jessica. I'll have to stay until morning, at least."

The travel feature! She'd forgotten it completely. As welcome as his company on the flight home would have been, Kayla could see it wasn't possible for Seth to drop everything and fly home.

At the airport, they bought Kayla a ticket to St. Louis. From there, she could catch a connecting flight and be in Milwaukee before midnight.

"You don't have to wait here with me. You've got some driving to do if you're going to catch up with Jessica," said Kayla, once arrangements were made.

"After what happened back at the restaurant, I'm not taking any chances." Seth waited with her until the plane prepared for take off. At the boarding gate, he held her a long moment. "Keep praying, you hear?"

Her vision blurred as she thought of her niece, so tiny and fragile and perfect. Seth's arms tightened. "I'll page you at the hospital around twelve-thirty. Maybe someone will know something by then. And Kayla?" He tipped up her face and kissed her. "I love you."

Tears spilled down her cheeks. "I love you, too."

"I never should have let you go the first time," he whispered.

The zipper tab of his leather jacket blurred. "Maybe it was for the best. Six months, a year down the road, you would have been off on some photo adventure that led to another and another, until you realized you didn't want to come home."

"It's equally possible neither one of us gave love enough credit." He couldn't quite admit she was right.

"Maybe," she agreed, heart hurting as he kissed her once more.

Reluctantly, he released her and gave her a nudge through the boarding gate, warning, "Be careful. We can't be sure Richard's not behind all that's happened. If Josh isn't free to look into it, you go to the sheriff, you hear?"

Early the next morning, a bleary-eyed Kayla caught a cab at the Milwaukee airport. The cab ride to the hospital seemed to take nearly as long as the flight. Once at the hospital, Kayla learned that Shelly and Joshua were in conference with a pediatric specialist. She found the pediatric wing and sat down in the lounge to wait.

Shelly and Joshua emerged from the conference room a short while later. Kayla sprang out of her chair. "How's Joy?"

"At the moment, she's doing fine." Shelly seemed too tired to be surprised by Kayla's unexpected appearance. Her bottom lip trembled, and brokenly, she added, "It was a different story a few hours ago! I checked on her right after supper, and she'd stopped breathing."

"Stopped breathing? You don't mean—"

"I've never been so scared in all my life." Battling for composure, Shelly entreated, "You tell her, Josh."

Josh was nearly as pale as Shelly. "The doctor had

a name for it, but I was too dazed to take it in. Simply put, something inside malfunctioned and Joy forgot to breath. If Shelly hadn't looked in on her, we might have lost her."

The terror of the situation gripped Kayla. "What did you do, Shelly?"

"I snatched her up out of the cradle and screamed for Josh. He dialed 911. Josh started shouting instructions to me as they came in over the phone. All I could do was shake."

"You did just fine," Josh soothed his wife. Eyes meeting Kayla's, he added, "Shelly kept her head, and in a matter of seconds, Joy was breathing again."

Kayla listened intently as Josh brought her up to date. "They'll watch her for the rest of the night, keeping a close eye on the monitor. Tomorrow, if all goes well, we can take her home."

"The doctor's sending a monitor home with us. He insists it's completely reliable and that it'll beep a warning if she should have any more difficulties," added Shelly.

"It may never happen again. But if it does, all we have to do is give her a shake, just enough to make her breathe," Josh added quietly.

What a nightmare! Under the circumstances, Kayla thought they were both holding up well. She passed Shelly a tissue and asked, "Have you seen her yet?"

Shelly nodded. "They've been good to let us spend five or ten minutes with her each hour."

Noting the dark circles under her sister's eyes, Kayla wondered when she'd last slept. Josh looked exhausted too. As they sat talking, a nurse came for Shelly. She flashed a comforting smile.

"Joy is crying for her mama. She says it's time to eat."

Shelly sprang out of her chair and followed the nurse.

Joshua rubbed red-rimmed eyes. "Let's get a cup of coffee."

They sat down at a table in the deserted coffee shop. Kayla spooned sugar into her tea as Josh sipped his steaming coffee.

"What's become of Seth?" asked Josh.

Kayla's heart jumped at his name and the memory of all that had happened in the hours preceding her flight home. She began with Seth's lighthearted message left on Richard's answering machine, held her composure through an account of her attack, and wound up with the ransacking of Seth's motor home.

Josh was a professional, not easily alarmed. But the more Kayla talked, the deeper the lines that concern drew on his face.

"I don't know what Farrell's mixed up in," he said when she finally fell silent. "Or if he has anything to do with what's happened to you. I do know that bank records, credit card records, that sort of thing tell a very different story than the modest income he's reporting to the IRS. Whatever he's doing, it's doubtful the money is coming through legal avenues."

"So he could have stolen the artifacts?" Kayla asked.

Josh nodded. "But we can't find any proof of it."

As Josh finished his coffee, Kayla told him about the certified letter. She asked, too, if there'd been any leads on the bald-headed man who'd come to the post office asking about Richard.

Josh shook his head. "But that could be who broke into Farrell's house on Friday night."

Kayla caught a surprised breath. "Richard's home was broken into?"

Josh nodded. "Seth was in such a hurry when he called, I forgot to mention it. Alert neighbors heard the prowler, knew Farrell was away, and called us. When we arrived on the scene, there was evidence of forced entry, but no prowler."

"It couldn't have been Misha?"

"The neighbors don't think so. They say she has an apartment in Milwaukee."

Kayla nodded. "She's a student at the university."

"Yes, but we had no luck getting in touch with her. Is it possible she accompanied Farrell on his trip out of town?"

"I don't think so, though, who knows? I haven't been right about anything concerning Richard so far." Kayla chewed her bottom lip a moment, then suggested, "Contact the university. Misha's professors will know whether or not she's been in class. And what about the IRS?"

"What about them?"

Kayla said, "Ask them about the certified letter. They should have received the green card back in the mail. The number on it would match the yellow signature slip filed at the post office."

"You think it's significant?"

"I don't know, Josh. It was just so odd—his eagerness to make it look as if he hadn't received it. I can't understand, with them having called on him in person, why he'd get so excited over a certified letter."

Josh scribbled himself a note. "I'll check it out."

"Did the prowler take anything?" Kayla asked.

"It looked as if a few things had been disturbed. But until we get a family member to go through the house, it's hard to say whether or not things were stolen."

"Come across any artifacts?" she asked.

Josh shook his head. "If he had them and they were stolen, we'll have nothing at all to tie Farrell to the looting at the burial grounds."

"If, indeed, he was involved."

The waitress came to refill their cups. When she had gone, they resumed their conversation.

"Right," Josh agreed. "But Farrell's association with the archeologist is curious, don't you think?"

Kayla nodded.

"And if it wasn't the artifacts, then we'll have to stay on the case until we figure out his game," added Josh.

It would have been nice if Kayla could have believed there was an explanation, that the IRS had somehow made a mistake. But her naivete concerning Richard had, over the past two days, become all too clear.

"By the way, Seth told me it was you who sent the picture of Richard's other woman," Kayla said. At Josh's sheepish look, she added, "Don't bother explaining. Seth told me it was your sensitive side."

Josh grimaced. "Sorry, Kayla. It probably wasn't the best way of handling it."

"Did you turn up anything on her?"

Josh shook his head and reached into his pocket. "We had this enlargement made of her face. Are you sure you've never seen her?"

Kayla studied the blow up of the woman's face. Some of the clarity had been lost in the enlargement process, making her features a little fuzzy. She studied it carefully. There was something about it, something familiar. Kayla scrutinized the face once again, then the jewelry. The earrings! That was it! She'd given Misha a pair just like them for Christmas.

"You aren't saying—" Josh began.

"No, no! It's not Misha. At least, I don't think it is. Misha doesn't have a mole on her face. Her eyes aren't that color. And her hair isn't that long. But those earrings!" Kayla paused. Misha was accustomed to lovely things, and when Christmas came, Kayla had gone all out. It was false pride, pure and simple, that prompted her to order custom earrings from a jeweler in Milwaukee.

"Those earrings are shark's teeth dipped in gold and embedded in circlets of mother-of-pearl. I had them made for Misha as a Christmas gift."

"Then you think it's Misha?"

Confused, Kayla said, "I don't know, Josh. If it's her, she's very well disguised. I can see no reason for that. Nor do I understand, if she did go on the trip with Richard, why she led me to believe otherwise."

Josh frowned. "I don't quite follow."

"I ran into her at the Maple Festival last weekend. She mentioned Richard being there, too. I said I hadn't realized he was home, and she said, 'Yes, he flew in this morning.' Not *we* flew in, but *he*. And Josh!" Kayla's voice climbed as another nugget dropped into place. "Misha was wearing the earrings! I remember feeling pleased that she liked them!"

"I'll call the department, tell them to take a harder look at the girl," said Josh as he rose to his feet.

On their return to pediatrics, Shelly sent Josh home to get some sleep. A kind-hearted nurse brought a fold-out cot into the small lounge beside the nursery where little Joy lay sleeping. At Kayla's urging, Shelly stretched out and was soon sound asleep.

Kayla sat quietly, thinking first of the baby, then of Seth, and finally of Richard. A week ago, he had seemed so central to her life. Now, here she was working piece by piece on the puzzle Richard had become.

Had he stolen Indian relics? If so, in what way was Misha involved? What about the man at the post office and the intruder who broke into Richard's house? Were they one and the same? And her attacker. What was his connection? As for Marion Stauffer, she would be knowledgeable about Indian artifacts. Could Richard have manipulated her in some way? Or was she a willing participant in the theft and, possibly, resale of the relics?

Unpleasant though it was to face, speculation that Richard was a skilled manipulator involving himself with women who were useful to him couldn't be ignored. In what way had he planned to use her? The certified letter drifted to mind. But she hadn't given into his request.

In thinking it over, Kayla realized that Richard often asked little favors, like using her depot for storage when the water problem developed in his basement. But that was no more than what any friend might ask of another.

Kayla wandered over to the nursery window and gazed at Kayla Joy. One tiny fist had escaped the securely wrapped blanket. She smiled tenderly as the baby's little red mouth opened in a yawn.

As Kayla sat down, the certified letter once more popped to mind. It was as if that inner voice kept waving it in front of her eyes, earmarking it as significant. She went over the whole thing again in her mind. Having signed for the piece, Richard clearly didn't want the IRS to know he'd received it. Why was that so important? What was in the letter? A bill for nonpayment or notification of an audit? But why would that upset him so? Unless. . . .

What if it wasn't from the IRS? The thought dropped out of nowhere. Kayla seized it for closer examination. She'd dated the green card and dropped it back into the mail. But she hadn't noticed if it went back to the IRS. It could have gone to a post office box anywhere in the country. Someone could have used the IRS envelope to mask their true business.

The idea seemed a little far-fetched, yet during her years with the post office, Kayla had come to realize unscrupulous people found all sorts of creative ways to use, abuse, and exploit the postal service.

So where did that leave her? Right where she'd started. Discouraged, Kayla turned her thoughts to the relics stolen from the archaeological dig. If Richard had taken them, where were they now? Had he smuggled them out of the country on one of his many business trips? Or did he still have them? And if so, where?

Suddenly, Kayla thought of the antique shop she'd visited that morning, the beautiful old furniture, and the cleverly concealed hiding places within each piece. She bolted out of her chair. Reluctant to awaken her exhausted sister, Kayla paused long enough to pin a note of explanation to Shelly's cot before she left.

twelve

It was four in the morning by the time the taxi dropped Kayla at her apartment. The phone was ringing when she walked in. Seth had said he'd call the hospital, but he hadn't. Thinking it might be him, she raced to get it. The answering machine clicked on just as Kayla reached the phone.

"Just a second," she said over the recorded message.

"You've got something that belongs to my client," a male voice spoke the moment the message ended.

Disappointed it wasn't Seth, the words went right over Kayla's head. Ready to dismiss the caller altogether, she said, "I'm afraid you have the wrong number."

"Shut up, lady, and listen!"

The man who'd dragged her out of the restaurant! Sudden recognition drove the air from Kayla's lungs as he growled, "My boss is out of patience. Bring the relics to St. Louis. There's a phone booth at Front and Kaskaskia Street. I'll call you there at six tonight. Any cops and your boyfriend gets it."

Kayla's knees went weak as Seth's voice spoke her name: "Kayla?"

"Seth? Where are you? Are you all right?"

"This fellow was waiting in the motor home at the airport. Do you know what this is all about?"

His voice was tightly controlled. No sign of fear, nor of the tender emotions he'd expressed earlier. Fearing the worst, panic brought the sting of tears. "Are you hurt? What've they done to you?"

"I told him he's got the wrong man, that you won't care what becomes of me. But he persists in thinking otherwise."

He was running a bluff! Before Kayla could respond, the guttural voice growled, "Six o'clock, if you want to see your boyfriend again. I'll tell you then how to make the exchange. No tricks, or Rattlesnake'll be sending you a letter."

Kayla gripped the phone tightly. "Put Seth on again," she pleaded, but the line went dead. Trembling, she sank into the nearest chair. The Indian relics! It had been about the relics all along! She hoped her hunch proved true, for if they weren't at the depot, she had nothing to exchange for Seth's life!

The wrong man, he'd said. Praying for calm, Kayla's nerves jumped as the recorder clicked off. She had the man's voice on tape! She'd call Josh. He'd know what to do.

Before she had the number dialed, Kayla changed her mind. The man had said no cops. If she didn't follow his instructions, he might kill Seth. Hands trembling, she rewound the tape. Seth's voice rushed over her.

The stolen relics. The man who'd attacked her,

searched the motor home, and now had Seth—it all had to do with the relics. And with Richard. The same man must be responsible for the break-in at Richard's house. He'd heard the message on Richard's machine. But had that, in itself, been enough?

The old highway was 2,400 miles long. He would have needed at least a description of the motor home to find them. Had someone innocently given him the information? Or had Richard deliberately set the man on their trail in an effort to get him off his back? If so, then he may have already taken the relics and fled town.

Praying for help, for wisdom, for Seth's safety, Kayla grabbed her keys. She'd search the depot. If the objects weren't there, she'd go straight to Josh.

If they were.... She raced to the car, clinging to the promise of the ninety-first Psalm.

The old depot at the edge of town had a dark and uninviting silhouette. The headlights of Kayla's car made a path across its gray, clapboard siding. Nerves tightly coiled, she was acutely conscious of ordinary noises. The slam of her car door, the ring of her shoes on the stone walk, the metallic click of the key in the lock, all seemed to echo much too loudly.

The light switch was behind the door. Kayla pushed it shut, stepped back, and ran her hand along the wall until she found it. The bare overhead bulb hadn't the wattage to fill the corners of the still room. Her pulse raced at breakneck speed as she made her way to the bed Richard had stored at one of end of the room. It closely resembled the one she and Seth had crawled beneath such a few hours ago.

Heart squeezing tightly as she remembered their lighthearted fun, Kayla examined the workmanship of the posts at the foot of the bed. The smooth richness of the wood was cool against her palm. The post appeared to have been hand-lathed in one piece, but her sensitive fingers found a small seam. She gripped the post firmly and pulled. It came free in her hand, revealing a hidden compartment about five inches in diameter.

At first glance, Kayla thought the space was empty. But as she reached in, her fingers grazed a foreign object. With great care, Kayla retrieved the object from its hiding place. It looked like the bowl of a ceremonial pipe. Shaped from stone, it was black with age.

The evidence of Richard's thievery in hand, Kayla wondered how many pieces made up the treasure. She'd have to find them all. Kayla pulled at the other posts on the bed, but without success. She rapped her knuckles against what appeared to be a solid walnut panel in a scrivener's desk. It rang hollow! After a bit of probing, Kayla found a tiny spring. The hidden compartment slid open, revealing an aged stone mortar and pestle. Despite the cool temperature in the depot, beads of perspiration slid down her temples.

There was only one more piece of furniture belonging to Richard. It was a four-shelf pie safe. She studied the dimensions a moment, suspecting a false bottom. A knock against the bottom panel confirmed it. After a bit of searching, she found the catch. The secret compartment contained a hodge-podge of arrowheads and small stone tools.

Kayla's hurried gaze roamed the room. Recalling the newspaper articles about the desecrated burial grounds, she felt certain there had to be more. *Please, God. Help me!* she prayed.

Richard had told her a good deal about the bed, but he hadn't mentioned the mirror. His omission fueled her hope. She took a pen-light from her pocketbook and crawled beneath the bed. Her heart leaped as the wavy glass she'd hoped to find threw back her reflection. But her joy was short-lived. If there were a deep compartment behind the glass, how was she to find the opening?

It took Kayla a good while to figure out how to fold the bed into itself. Upright, the bed looked like a wardrobe with a mirrored door. And the door—yes! Jackpot!

Inside, carefully wrapped and secured, was a varied assortment of artifacts. Kayla didn't take time to unwrap and identify them; rather, she found an empty crate and carefully stashed everything inside.

A cold sky was turning shades of night to dawn as Kayla switched out the light and locked the door behind her. Her legs ached with weariness as she started toward her car. She had her hand on the door when a twig snapped on the path behind her. She whirled around as Richard stepped out of the shadows. All the air rushed from her lungs. His name came out an agonized whisper.

"Well, well. Look who's back," his tone mocked. A nerve jerked along his cheekbone as he sent a furtive glance down the deserted street. "You were the one woman I was sure I could count on. And what do you do? Run off with your old boyfriend, then sneak back and steal what belongs to me."

Fear squeezed Kayla's chest. The words in her head as Richard reached to take the crate from her were repetitive pleas for deliverance. Resisting, she stumbled back a step. "Josh knows I'm here. He's on his way."

"Then you'd better make it snappy, hadn't you?" Richard's terse reply was accompanied by a smooth motion of his hand into his coat.

Kayla backed away from the gleaming revolver.

"My car's behind the building. Easy, no quick moves." He stepped behind her, prodding with the snubbed barrel of the gun.

Kayla edged toward the back of the building, Richard right behind, pushing her along. He motioned for her to get into the car. All her training screamed warnings. "No," she said firmly. "I'm not going anywhere with you."

Richard pressed the barrel of the gun against her face. She flinched as the cold steel chilled her skin, but she made no move to get into the car.

"You're a smart woman. Use your head," he hissed.

"What is it you want, Richard?" Kayla feigned a

steely calm.

"Your cooperation. I've got a collector out on the West Coast waiting for these trinkets."

"There's a man in St. Louis who wants them, too. If he doesn't get them, Seth Brooks may die."

Richard's low laugh chilled her blood. "Forget Seth Brooks. We can make a fresh start, you and I. I'm a forgiving kind of guy. Just say the word, and I'll forget this little misunderstanding."

Kayla closed her eyes, afraid he'd see just how repugnant he'd become in her sight. He wasn't in love with her; he'd counted on her being useful. And if she proved not to be, killing her would be no hardship. *Please, Lord, give me courage, give me words.*

As Kayla opened her eyes, she caught a reflection in the bushes behind Richard. Josh, armed and in uniform, emerged from the shadows. He put a warning finger to his lips.

Words came, words to prolong the conversation and give Josh needed time. Kayla asked Richard about Misha.

Richard's eyes narrowed. "What about her?"

"She's never liked me. What makes you think she'd accept me now?"

"I'm her father, she'll do what I say."

"And what about Marion Stauffer?"

Richard said shortly, "Marion's blind about everything but her work. She knows who owns what, what it's worth, where's it's stored."

"She was in on the theft?"

"At the burial grounds?" Richard snorted. "Marion's straight as an arrow. She loves to talk shop—that's what makes her so useful."

"People can be swayed, though," Kayla said. "You must believe that, or you wouldn't be wasting your time on me. Am I right, Richard?"

"It's not like that with you," he protested. "I have deep feelings."

"So deep, you've got a gun on me," Kayla said. "Just out of curiosity, what do you need me for, anyway?"

"There are times a friend in the post office would come in handy. Come to the airport with me. We'll have all the time in the world to talk."

"Is Misha waiting there?" asked Kayla, stalling as Josh inched up behind Richard.

"She took off. The break-in spooked her," said Richard. "She was alone in the house. Fast talking on her part convinced Rattlesnake's henchmen that you'd double-crossed me and taken off with the artifacts. You always did underestimate her, you know."

"So it was Misha who sent them after us!"

"That, and the message Brooks left on my machine. Couldn't have been more perfectly worded." Richard's calculating smile gleamed in the fading darkness. "I'm out of time, Kayla. Are you coming willingly, or do I have to"

He never got a chance to finish the sentence. Josh struck him from behind. The force of the blow sent Richard sprawling to the ground. Kayla helped hold

Richard down as Josh snapped handcuffs on his wrists. He patted him down and called, "All clear."

The sheriff and a deputy rushed forward. Seeing Josh had the situation well in hand, they put their guns away. Aftershocks rumbled through Kayla. She passed over the box of artifacts and leaned against the car, trembling.

Josh draped a supportive arm over her shoulder. "You okay?"

She swallowed the lump in her throat and nodded. "How'd you find me?"

"Shelly woke up, read the note, and called me."

Tears burned as Kayla said in a rush, "Josh, Seth's been kidnapped! We have to get these artifacts to St. Louis by six tonight, or they'll kill him."

"Whoa, slow down." Josh guided her back inside the depot and eased her gently into a chair. "Take a deep breath. That's better. Okay. What's this about Seth?"

The sheriff read Richard his rights, then took him back to the station. Having heard Kayla's story, Josh took her along to the station with him, where she repeated all that she knew to the sheriff.

The sheriff picked up the phone and alerted federal authorities. They arrived within the hour to interview Kayla. When she'd told them all she could, they sent her home, insisting they'd take care of everything.

It had been twenty-four hours since Kayla had had any sleep. Every muscle in her body ached. But she couldn't rest until she'd booked a flight to St. Louis.

If Seth hadn't been found by early afternoon, she'd convince the agents to let her exchange the relics for his safe return. But she was going to have to get some rest first. She was too tired to think.

After a hot soothing bath, Kayla curled up on the sofa and drifted to sleep praying the federal agents would rescue Seth soon and the whole ordeal would be over.

But it was not to be. Josh and the agents showed up at Kayla's door, awakening her around noon. Kayla asked first about the baby, and on hearing Shelly was preparing to bring her home, breathed a prayer of thanksgiving.

Returning to the business at hand, Josh and the agents took turns bringing Kayla up to date. They'd been in contact with the police as well as their counterparts in the St. Louis area, and although they'd located Seth's motor home at the Springfield, Missouri, airport they'd found no trace of Seth.

"Is Richard talking?" asked Kayla, her empty stomach a tangle of raw nerves.

"Not yet," said Josh. "We have learned a good deal about Misha Farrell, though. The university had no record of her, so we lifted her fingerprints at the house and ran them through the national network."

"Misha Farrell is an alias for Marie La Rauche, twice tried for stealing antiquities from private collectors," said the older of the two agents.

"But never convicted." A tall, blond, ruddy-faced fellow straightened his tie. "She's currently being sought for questioning concerning some eighteenth-century paintings stolen from a collector in New York and is a master at disguising herself."

"Reproductions of the paintings have surfaced around the country, each having been purchased with the belief it was an original." The second agent smoothed graying hair and settled his ample frame more comfortably into the chair.

"Then she's an artist?" asked Kayla, surprised.

"No. She has connections with someone who is. Networking is the key, even in the con business."

The blond agent waved aside Kayla's offer to make coffee and picked up the story. "According to her dossier, she's in her mid-twenties, been divorced three times, and is rumored to be living with a man named Bradford Bentley, alias—"

"Richard Farrell?" Kayla chimed in.

Josh nodded. "They're partners, Kayla, as well as lovers."

"I should have known they weren't father and daughter. She was hostile toward me from the very beginning. No wonder!" Kayla's head ached from too little sleep. She massaged throbbing temples. "But I still don't understand why Richard thought I'd be useful to him."

"He came to town a stranger," Josh reminded her. "Misha was on the run. They both needed a cloak of respectability, and you gave it to them. Also, Richard may have had nefarious plans for your depot farther on down the road."

Too tired to feel the sting of humiliation, Kayla looked from Josh to the agents. "I think Richard knows where she is."

"No doubt. And who knows? When he's had time to think, he may lead us right to her rather than take the fall by himself," said the older agent.

Kayla came to her feet, fear for Seth gnawing a raw place in her stomach. "I made a plane reservation in the event you didn't find Seth. I'm going to be at that phone booth at six."

"Take it easy, Miss Colter," said the portly, gray-haired agent. "We're leaving for St. Louis within the hour. If Brooks hasn't been located by the time the phone call comes, we'll use the artifacts to gain his release."

"I'll fly down with you," said Kayla. Seeing the agents exchange guarded glances, she looked to Josh for support. "The man on the phone said for me to be there, Josh. He knows my voice! He knows my face. I'm going to follow his instructions to the letter."

"We anticipated you might feel that way," admitted the older agent. "Taking into consideration your background in police work, it is a possibility. And certainly, you can come along and take the phone call. But quite frankly, I'd rather one of our people handle the drop."

Kayla drew upon the best of her training and maintained a level manner as she presented her argument. Though they didn't tell her she could do it, she could see they were considering the possibility as

Josh filled her in on a few more details.

"I checked out the certified letter, Kayla, just as you suggested. The IRS had no record of having sent it. So I got a search warrant and went through Farrell's desk at work."

Pulse quickening, Kayla asked, "You found the letter?"

He nodded and rubbed tired eyes. "It was a plain sheet of paper containing one sentence: 'You've got one week from the date of receipt.'"

"Any idea what that means?" Kayla crossed back to her chair and perched on the edge of it.

"We've been working on it," said Josh. "According to key sources, there's a thug on the East Coast who is known for such letters. Rather nasty fellow."

"Goes by the name Rattlesnake," inserted one of the agents.

"Richard used that very name! And the man who called, he used it, too. He said I'd better cooperate, or Rattlesnake would send me a letter, too." She raced to the answering machine and played the message for the men.

Face grim, the older agent said, "It's not a threat to be taken lightly, Miss Colter. The guy is deadly."

"Who is he?" asked Kayla.

"A collector of Indian artifacts and a hoodlum. He got his nickname from his attribute of giving warning before he strikes. The warning comes in letter form."

"Sent certified mail."

Gooseflesh prickled the length of Kayla's arms.

Absorbing the information, she pieced it together. "Richard sold him reproductions instead of genuine artifacts and he wasn't fooled."

The agents and Josh seemed in general agreement that such an explanation would explain the warning.

"That might also explain Richard's last business trip."

"You think he'd sold some things and had to get them back for this Rattlesnake character?" asked Kayla.

"Either that, or whoever was making the reproductions was using the genuine article to make his work appear as authentic as possible."

Josh nodded. "That's probably it. Though, if Richard had done his homework on Rattlesnake, he'd have realized it was too late to make amends."

"What do you mean?"

"Once he's given warning, there's no stopping retribution," explained the sandy-haired agent.

"Farrell probably didn't realize that until he was in too deep," said his partner. "He may have thought the letter meant Rattlesnake would come in five days to collect the relics. He moved his furniture into your depot, planning to fetch the relics from wherever he'd stashed them and hide them close at hand. But after returning from his trip and stashing the relics, Farrell went home, saw the house had been trashed, and that Misha was gone."

"And it spooked him," the first agent theorized.

"Maybe. Or maybe he had no intentions of turning

them over to Rattlesnake. Maybe his intention was to skip town and send for his furniture when things cooled down," said Josh. He stirred restlessly and looked at his watch. "We may never know for sure unless we get a confession. One thing we do know— Richard was in way over his head."

Kayla paced to the front window facing south. The sparkle of sunlight on melting snow seemed a mockery of the dark fear within. Miles and miles away, Seth was in trouble. The responsibility was hers, and if she failed, she might lose him forever. Surely, God had not brought him back into her life for such a tragic end.

After a moment, she turned back, studied the men solemnly, and said, "This man holding Seth is probably the same man who came into the post office that day. He saw my face then, and again when he grabbed me in the restaurant. And he knows my voice. A substitute won't work. I have to make the drop; that's all there is to it."

thirteen

Josh accompanied Kayla and the two agents to St. Louis. They were met at the airport by another FBI agent and a police detective, a woman named Iva Harrison. Agent Jakes, a tall, lanky man with a thin, intense expression, had been in communication with the Milwaukee office throughout the day. He was aware that Kayla was determined to take the phone call as well as make the drop herself. It was clear he didn't care for the plan, even as he accepted it.

Detective Harrison drove them to a vacant office on Kaskaskia Street. They settled inside, spending what time remained finalizing plans. The office was in view of the phone booth where the call was to come in. There was a tap on the phone, and officers with sophisticated equipment were standing by in a van to monitor the call.

But it was God, not men, in whom Kayla put her trust as she stepped into the booth just minutes before six o'clock. She reached for the phone on the first ring. They had gone over and over the plan. She winged another prayer, then lifted the receiver and said without preamble, "Before you say a word, I want to talk to you about Richard Farrell."

"Shut up, lady, and listen."

"No, you listen. I've got what you want. But there's going to be some terms."

"Yes, and I'm making them," he cut her off. "Be at the east side of the Chain of Rocks Bridge in one hour, and we'll trade relics for boyfriend."

"If you mean Seth Brooks, he isn't my boyfriend," she retorted, heart quaking at the thought of that eerie old bridge.

"No cops."

"Wait a minute! I'm not from around here," Kayla protested, every breath a prayer. "I don't know if I can get there in an hour. I don't even know if I can *find* this. . .this bridge."

"Ask directions, lady. There's a hole in the fence. Park there and wait."

"Don't hang up. Not until you've heard what I have to say." Kayla tried to stretch out the call in hopes the agents could trace it and rescue Seth without having to play the scenario out to the end.

"Make it snappy."

"Mr. Brooks has nothing to do with my coming. He's here with a film crew, doing a piece on Route 66. He knows nothing about the relics. It's Richard Farrell I'm concerned about. I want to negotiate"

The line went dead.

Kayla exited the booth, fear mingling with frustration. No way could they have traced the call. She hadn't stretched it out long enough. Nor had she made any headway with her ruse, intended to convince Seth's kidnapper his pawn was of no value to her.

Immediately, Agent Jakes sent a surveillance team to comb the area on the east side of the Chain of Rocks Bridge. They were en route when the report came in that the team had arrived and the place was deserted.

"How about the bridge?" Jakes asked.

"We've got a man on it right now. But there may not be enough time. And it's dangerous in the dark."

"Very well. Stay well out of sight and keep alert. He sniffs us out and we'll have a mess on our hands," Jakes radioed back.

The interstate passed within a stone's throw of the old alignment where Kayla was to meet Seth's captor. They cruised down it, passing the site twice as they awaited the appointed hour.

With the clock ticking down, the short-wave radio crackled once more. A white rental car had driven down the old road and parked back in the trees within walking distance of the bridge. As far as the officers could tell, there was only one occupant.

Kayla drew a quick breath. Where was Seth?

"Easy. Don't panic," Josh soothed, though nervous himself. "God's looking after him."

Mutely, Kayla nodded, but from that moment on, she couldn't get warm. With only five minutes remaining, Agent Jakes pulled off the road half a mile from the meeting place.

"Stay in the car, doors locked, motor running, and the headlights on," he told her as Agent Harrison climbed out. "We want to be able to see you. Don't let him lure you into the woods, or out on the bridge, or into his vehicle," Jakes added.

Kayla nodded her understanding. Josh set the crate of artifacts on the seat next to her and squeezed her hand before climbing out.

This had to be every bit as difficult for him if not worse. Seth was his only brother. Kayla thought of Shelly and the baby and all that had happened in the last twenty-four hours and marveled at Josh's sustaining faith in the face of such difficult circumstances.

"Keep him talking as long as you can," Jakes continued. "If Mr. Brooks is in the car, we'll do our best to free him. If we can do so without attracting the kidnapper's attention, we'll give a bird call. That'll be your signal to turn the crate over and scram. We'll take it from there."

"And if you don't find Seth?" asked Kayla, though they'd been over that, too.

"It'll be trickier. You'll have to hang tough. Use your wits to negotiate, like I told you."

"You all right?" Josh asked. At Kayla's nod, he reached through the yawning door and gripped her hands once more. "Keep the faith."

"You've got lots of back-up," Jakes assured her. "There're men posted along the road, along the river bank, and in the woods."

Kayla gave a terse nod. Having mustered the courage, she wanted to get on with it. "May I go now?"

Jakes stepped back from the car. "Keep your chin up, Miss Colter. We'll do all we can to get Mr. Brooks back safely."

Praying to that end, Kayla eased the car into gear. The road was dark and deserted and riddled with potholes. She drove very slowly, searching for the fence in the darkness. It seemed she'd gone a great distance before she spotted it. There was no sign of the white car, but she could almost feel the kidnapper watching, waiting. It made the hair on her neck rise.

Barely making out the hole in the fence, Kayla stopped. There were no birds singing now. A minute passed. Two. Five. Ten. Beads of perspiration slid down her neck. The quiet was so intense, her heart sounded like war drums. Her nerves jumped at the sound of a stick snapping. A man took shape by her window. He rapped on the glass.

"Shut off your car."

His voice picked at the ice she'd become, showering chips through her veins. *Her fortress, her protector, her Savior.* She lowered the window a crack with a cold, clammy hand. "I'd rather leave it running."

"Shut up and do what I say. Your boyfriend's out there on the bridge. One wrong move and I'll bring it down."

Making no move to comply, Kayla returned in a level tone, "My boyfriend is back in Kitterly. That's what I was trying to tell you on the phone."

A flashlight beamed through the glass. She squinted and shaded her face against the glare. "Don't play games with me, lady. That fella out on the bridge is the only reason you're here. You two ran off together, and we both know it. Now give me the loot, and let's get on with it."

"Not so fast," said Kayla, pulse roaring in her ears. "Despite what you think, I didn't come because of Seth Brooks. I came because of Richard Farrell and the letter from your boss. Richard's an innocent. He thinks, once this fellow Rattlesnake gets his artifacts, that he'll forget their misunderstanding. But that's not how it works, is it?"

The man flicked off the flashlight and said in a hard voice, "Farrell's as good as dead."

"I was afraid of that. That's why I came. I want to negotiate for Richard Farrell's life."

He gave a raw, humorless laugh. "Lady, even if I believed you, you've got nothing to negotiate with."

"That's not true. I've got the artifacts, and I'm in touch with an entire network of useful people," Kayla said.

"Like who?"

"An archaeologist who knows all about priceless collections, both public and private. And Misha. She can get more relics like these. She's can melt through any security system," Kayla said, praying this bluff she was running didn't backfire and cost her her life as well as Seth's.

"You mean Maria La Rauche? She's good all right," he said, like a craftsman admiring an accomplished peer. "But, since she got mixed up with Farrell, she's too hot to touch."

"That's why Richard's useful to your boss," Kayla improvised. "He's willing to run the risk."

"Farrell's an idiot," he scoffed. "He proved that when he let you steal his treasure right from beneath his nose and run off with your old boyfriend."

"That's not what happened. And anyway, you're wrong about Maria. Richard has powers of persuasion with her. She'll help him if he asks her to," said Kayla.

"Yeah, right. And you'd welcome her help, knowing how it was with her and Farrell?"

Kayla said tersely, "I'll do whatever it takes to save Richard."

The man grunted his disgust. He shone the light through the window, dancing it over the crate of artifacts. Kayla saw the remote control detonator in his right hand. Two phrases echoed in her ears: "Your boyfriend's out there on the bridge" and "Bring it down." He was going to blow up the bridge and Seth with it! The ice she'd become splintered and rained shrapnel, piercing her heart. He wasn't bluffing; there was a bomb!

The beam of light danced over the artifacts. "Hand 'em over," he ordered.

"After we've discussed this further." The calm, like the words, came from somewhere outside of Kayla. "Or aren't you authorized to negotiate on Rattlesnake's behalf?"

"Lady, you're starting to irritate me."

"If your boss won't revoke his death sentence on Richard, then I'm taking my loot and I'm getting out of here." The light went off again. The detonator disappeared into the man's pocket. Cellophane crinkled as he opened a package of cigarettes. "You're so gung-ho on a deal, how about a show of faith?"

"What do you have in mind?" Kayla asked guardedly.

He shoved his hand into his pocket and withdrew the detonator. It lay in his open palm. "Button pushing, that's all."

Kayla forced words past the fear that rose in her throat. "Why bring that kind of heat on myself when there's nothing in it for me?"

"You were the one wanting a favor. Favors come at a high premium." He jiggled the thing in his hand. "Go on. Roll down the window and take it."

It mattered not what Agent Jakes had said or what prudence demanded. That detonator was Seth's lifeline. Kayla lowered the window and closed her fingers around it. Her hand shook as if she held Seth's beating heart within it.

A match flared as Seth's kidnapper lit his cigarette, illuminating the cruel curl of his lips. "Go ahead, hit the button. Or don't you have the stomach for it? I knew you were bluffing!"

He thrust his hand through the window. With her first instinct to keep him from wrenching the detonator away, Kayla was slow to realize his true intent. Too late, she saw one hand release the lock as the other jerked the car door open. She cried out in alarm as he lunged toward her, but before he could reach her, a shot rang out.

The man screamed in pain as a bullet tore into his shoulder. His face contorted. He gripped the wound, swayed, and fell into the car. Kayla recoiled and pushed him away, then swooned at the warm sticky smear of blood on her hand. Head reeling, vision blurring, she fell forward. The world tipped as her head hit the horn. But above the blare of it, an explosion rumbled, shaking the earth and lighting the night sky with fire and smoke.

The bridge! Seth, Seth! Her soul screamed his name as she surrendered to the dull gray web of unconsciousness.

"Miss Colter?"

"She's coming around."

"Kayla? Open your eyes. That a girl."

Josh and Detective Harrison were crowded in the car door, trying to rouse Kayla from her stupor. As the gray fuzz faded, Kayla's thoughts picked up where they'd left off.

The terrifying events rushed over her with alarming clarity. The smell of fuel and smoke burned her throat. She could hear the flames licking. The bridge! She'd fallen on the remote and blown up the bridge! Seth was gone! Her heart shattered. She clutched at the only familiar hand.

"Seth! He was on the bridge!"

Joshua's hands closed around hers. "Easy, Kayla.

Everything's fine."

"You don't understand! He was on the bridge!" she cried again.

"He's all right, Kayla. We got him out in time. Seth's all right." Josh's words rushed over her.

Relief brought a flood of tears. "Where is he? I want to see him!"

"He's got a gash on his head. They're keeping him still just in case of a concussion," Josh explained. "An ambulance is on the way."

"I fell on the remote! I blew up the bridge! Josh, I nearly killed him!"

"He wasn't on the bridge; he was in the trunk of the kidnapper's car," said Josh. "That's what exploded, not the bridge. The kidnapper wired a bomb to the car. Once he got those artifacts, he didn't plan on leaving any witnesses."

Trembling in the aftermath, Kayla struggled to get out of the car, to go to Seth, but Detective Harrison slid in beside her, blocking her way. She gripped her hand warmly.

"Congratulations, Miss Colter. You did a fine job. You kept the kidnapper occupied long enough for us to free Mr. Brooks."

"Is he dead?"

"The kidnapper? No. Agent Jakes caught him in the shoulder. He'll live to testify," the young detective assured her.

"And Seth's all right? He's really all right?"

"He's just fine, thanks to you. Agent Jakes is eating crow. He never would have let you do this if it hadn't been for your training." Detective Harrison added with a wry smile, "Though I've got to wonder, how'd a gal who faints at the sight of blood ever hold down a job as a cop?"

Kayla rested her head against the seat. She framed a tired smile. "I have friends in High Places." *Thank You, sweet Lord. My refuge, my fortress, my God in whom I Trust.*

Kayla spent what remained of the night in a St. Louis hospital where Seth had been admitted for observation. The kidnapper, who'd followed them to the airport, had armed himself with a walking stick he'd found in the motor home. It was the stick and the struggle that had ensued which accounted for Seth's gashes and bumps and bruises. Fortunately, the doctor found no evidence of a concussion. If all went well, Seth could leave the hospital the following day.

A reporter turned up, just as Seth was being wheeled from emergency care to a shared room on the second floor. For the first time, Kayla thought of Jessica Williams and Mark. Jessica was probably in a dither, wondering what had become of them.

Seth, concerned too, suggested, "Call Jessica's station in Chicago. They'll know how to get in touch with her. I should be getting out of here in the morning. If I drive hard all day, I can catch up with her."

It was the gypsy in him, of course. He'd always be a rover. She needn't think she could change him.

But doubts were gone. They could be one, like Lowell and Anna, as they dwelt together in the shelter of the Most High.

There were both local and federal law enforcement officers in the room, wanting to talk with Seth, so Kayla found a pay phone to make the call. Because of the lateness of the hour, she had no luck reaching anyone at the station. The best she could do was to leave a message on their machine.

Kayla returned to Seth's room to find he was still being interviewed. The nurse who came in on Kayla's heels took a narrow view of all the company. She was concerned they'd disturb the patient in the other bed. So Kayla found a chair at the end of the corridor and waited for the traffic to thin.

Josh, who had gotten in touch with the sheriff back in Kitterly, joined her there. He'd learned that Richard had made a full confession. He had, with Misha's help, stolen the artifacts from Professor Stauffer's field office where they'd been stored during the dig for safekeeping. The professor, herself, was innocent of any wrongdoing, other than being enamored with Richard and being too trusting. As for Misha, she'd been arrested out on the East Coast as had the kidnapper's boss, Rattlesnake.

Josh had also called Shelly.

"How's the baby?" Kayla asked anxiously.

"She's home and doing just fine. Shelly's a little nervous about the monitor, though." Josh rubbed tired eyes and added, "I called the airport. There's a flight home in an hour. You coming with me?"

Home, with all it's cozy associations, sounded wonderful. Yet there was a stronger pull, and Kayla yielded to it. "I've got to see Seth, first. But tell Shelly I'll be home soon."

It was late by the time Seth's visitors all left. Kayla stole up to the bed, his wholeness so precious after all they'd been through. Tears stung the back of her eyelids as he winced and touched his bandaged head.

"That fella packed a mean wallop," he complained.

Kayla covered his hand with her own. "I still don't understand why he nabbed you."

"I figure he followed us last night, hoping we'd lead him to the relics. He knew from his search that they weren't in the motor home."

Seth's fingers closed around hers. "When we wound up at the airport, he may have thought we'd had them shipped in and were picking them up. Or maybe he thought we were meeting someone who'd have them."

"Like Richard?"

Seth nodded. "He couldn't figure out where I fit in, yet he wasn't willing to accept that I didn't. So when I returned to the motor home alone and without the relics, I was all he had. It was a gamble on his part, holding me in hopes of negotiating for the treasure."

Kayla smoothed the covers with her free hand. "I guess we'll never know exactly what was going through his mind unless he chooses to tell someone."

Seth rested against the pillow. His gaze followed her as she let go of his hand and slipped into the chair nearest the bed. "Thanks, by the way, for your part in saving my life. Detective Harrison said you were cool under pressure."

"If you overlook the fact that I nearly killed you myself, fainting on that remote!" A catch in her voice, Kayla added, "Thank God you were out of that trunk when it blew."

"He'd have blown up the car himself if he'd gotten the chance. He didn't want to leave any witnesses. If Jakes hadn't picked him off, he would have killed you, too."

Kayla shivered, knowing it was true. "I hope they can make criminal charges stick to the guy—and his boss, too."

"It remains to be proven whether or not Rattlesnake had anything to do with my kidnapping," Seth reminded her.

"But he did put out a contract on Richard's life."

Seth adopted a tragic expression and quipped, "Richard again, is it? I don't know. After all this, I'd think you'd have him on a hit list of your own."

Color rising, Kayla wandered to the end of the bed and stood looking back at Seth. "It's incredible, really. How could I have been so blind?"

A gentle smile graced his bruised face. "Love is supposed to be blind. At least that's what poets and wise men say."

"I wasn't in love with Richard." Finding it hard to put into words, Kayla turned toward the dark window. No one had bothered to draw the blinds. The lights of the city twinkled below. She admitted in a low voice, "And yet, in the back of my mind, there was this idea that maybe, in time, we'd settle down together."

"You and Richard and Misha. There's a grim thought," said Seth, gentle mockery in his tone.

Kayla nodded, keeping her back to him as she admitted, "I guess what worries me the most is that I was willing to settle for less than what I really want from life."

"Which is?" he challenged softly.

She started at the closeness of his voice and turned to find him standing just behind her. Distracted, she murmured, "You're supposed to be in bed."

He rested his chin on top of her head. His arms encircled her loosely. "Can't help myself. I don't want to miss a word of this. You were about to tell me what it is you want."

The back of her head fit snugly against his shoulder. His arms were warm as they linked around hers. She rested against him, wanting him— all of him—forever. "What Lowell and Anna have. That oneness. That sharing."

Seth's unshaven cheek prickled her fair skin as he pressed his face to hers. "Have I got an adventure for you!"

She framed a tired smile and admitted, "I'm not

sure I have the constitution for adventure."

"Oh, I don't know. You were right in the thick of it," he reminded.

"Just a quiet little life by the side of the road," she continued, ignoring his comments.

"You're doing it again. Asking for too little. God is willing and able to give abundant gifts." Seth wagged his head as if her lack of imagination disappointed him.

She turned in his arms, a soft laugh between them. "My, that's quite an opinion you have of yourself."

The whiskery stitches lent Seth a rakish appeal as he grinned and retorted, "It's taken a real battering here lately. If I'm such a catch, how come I'm having all this trouble getting you to the altar?"

"Seven year detours." She tipped her face, a kiss waiting for him.

He was quick to claim it, forgetting in his eagerness that his mouth was bruised. Wincing, he tried it a second time, then murmured, "That's good nursing. You've missed your calling."

With boldness born of a very long wait, Kayla smiled and said, "No I haven't. My calling is you."

His eyes swept over her face, full of tenderness and longing. "In that case, let's buy a license tomorrow. We'll get married right away."

"Can't. Not for another week or so, anyway. It's not on Jessica's itinerary."

Seth laughed and pulled her close again, saying, "Come here, you." He kissed her gingerly, then said on a wistful note, "You're going home, aren't you?"

She nodded. "I have to. I have a wedding to plan."

"Can't talk you into going the whole route first?" he entreated.

"With Jessica? No thanks."

He laughed, his blue gaze searching her face as if he missed her already. "I'll get the job done and be back to Kitterly in no time. Then we'll go down this old lover's lane again, just the two of us—like Lowell and Anna. What do you say?"

Kayla said it all, said it best, said it forever, with a kiss.

A Letter To Our Readers

Dear Reader:

In order that we might better contribute to your reading enjoyment, we would appreciate your taking a few minutes to respond to the following questions. When completed, please return to the following:

Rebecca Germany, Editor
Heartsong Presents
P.O. Box 719
Uhrichsville, Ohio 44683

1. Did you enjoy reading *Picture Perfect*?
   ☐ Very much. I would like to see more books by this author!
   ☐ Moderately
   I would have enjoyed it more if _____

   _____

2. Are you a member of *Heartsong Presents*? Yes   No
   If no, where did you purchase this book? _____

   _____

3. What influenced your decision to purchase this book? (Circle those that apply.)

Cover	Back cover copy
Title	Friends
Publicity	Other _____

4. On a scale from 1 (poor) to 10 (superior), please rate the following elements.

    ___Heroine   ___Plot

    ___Hero   ___Inspirational theme

    ___Setting   ___Secondary characters

5. What settings would you like to see covered in *Heartsong Presents* books?

   _____

   _____

6. What are some inspirational themes you would like to see treated in future books?_____

   _____

   _____

7. Would you be interested in reading other *Heartsong Presents* titles?   Yes   No

8. Please circle your age range:

Under 18	18-24	25-34
35-45	46-55	Over 55

9. How many hours per week do you read? _____

Name _____

Occupation _____

Address _____

City _____ State _____ Zip _____

······ Heartsong ·····

ROMANCE IS CHEAPER BY THE DOZEN!

Any 12 *Heartsong Presents* titles for only $26.95 *

Buy any assortment of twelve *Heartsong Presents* titles and save 25 % off of the already discounted price of $2.95 each!

*plus $1.00 shipping and handling per order and sales tax where applicable.

HEARTSONG PRESENTS TITLES AVAILABLE NOW:

____HP 1   A TORCH FOR TRINITY, *Colleen L. Reece*
____HP 2   WILDFLOWER HARVEST, *Colleen L. Reece*
____HP 3   RESTORE THE JOY, *Sara Mitchell*
____HP 4   REFLECTIONS OF THE HEART, *Sally Laity*
____HP 5   THIS TREMBLING CUP, *Marlene Chase*
____HP 6   THE OTHER SIDE OF SILENCE, *Marlene Chase*
____HP 7   CANDLESHINE, *Colleen L. Reece*
____HP 8   DESERT ROSE, *Colleen L. Reece*
____HP 9   HEARTSTRINGS, *Irene B. Brand*
____HP10 SONG OF LAUGHTER, *Lauraine Snelling*
____HP11 RIVER OF FIRE, *Jacquelyn Cook*
____HP12 COTTONWOOD DREAMS, *Norene Morris*
____HP13 PASSAGE OF THE HEART, *Kjersti Hoff Baez*
____HP14 A MATTER OF CHOICE, *Susannah Hayden*
____HP15 WHISPERS ON THE WIND, *Maryn Langer*
____HP16 SILENCE IN THE SAGE, *Colleen L. Reece*
____HP17 LLAMA LADY, *VeraLee Wiggins*
____HP18 ESCORT HOMEWARD, *Eileen M. Berger*
____HP19 A PLACE TO BELONG, *Janelle Jamison*
____HP20 SHORES OF PROMISE, *Kate Blackwell*
____HP21 GENTLE PERSUASION, *Veda Boyd Jones*
____HP22 INDY GIRL, *Brenda Bancroft*
____HP23 GONE WEST, *Kathleen Karr*
____HP24 WHISPERS IN THE WILDERNESS, *Colleen L. Reece*
____HP25 REBAR, *Mary Carpenter Reid*
____HP26 MOUNTAIN HOUSE, *Mary Louise Colln*
____HP27 BEYOND THE SEARCHING RIVER *Jacquelyn Cook*
____HP28 DAKOTA DAWN, *Lauraine Snelling*
____HP29 FROM THE HEART, *Sara Mitchell*
____HP30 A LOVE MEANT TO BE, *Brenda Bancroft*
____HP31 DREAM SPINNER, *Sally Laity*
____HP32 THE PROMISED LAND, *Kathleen Karr*
____HP33 SWEET SHELTER, *VeraLee Wiggins*
____HP34 UNDER A TEXAS SKY, *Veda Boyd Jones*
____HP35 WHEN COMES THE DAWN, *Brenda Bancroft*
____HP36 THE SURE PROMISE, *JoAnn A. Grote*
____HP37 DRUMS OF SHELOMOH, *Yvonne Lehman*
____HP38 A PLACE TO CALL HOME, *Eileen M. Berger*
____HP39 RAINBOW HARVEST, *Norene Morris*
____HP40 PERFECT LOVE, *Janelle Jamison*

(If ordering from this page, please remember to include it with the order form.)

·········Presents·········

Great Inspirational Romance at a Great Price!

Heartsong Presents books are inspirational romances in contemporary and historical settings, designed to give you an enjoyable, spirit-lifting reading experience. You can choose from 60 wonderfully written titles from some of today's best authors like Lauraine Snelling, Brenda Bancroft, Sara Mitchell, and many others.

When ordering quantities less than twelve, above titles are $2.95 each.

SEND TO: Heartsong Presents Reader's Service
          P.O. Box 719, Uhrichsville, Ohio 44683

Please send me the items checked above. I am enclosing $_____
(please add $1.00 to cover postage per order. OH add 6.5% tax. PA and NJ add 6%.). Send check or money order, no cash or C.O.D.s, please.
    To place a credit card order, call 1-800-847-8270.

NAME _____

ADDRESS _____

CITY/STATE _____ ZIP_____

LOVE A GREAT LOVE STORY?
Introducing Heartsong Presents —
Your Inspirational Book Club

Heartsong Presents Christian romance reader's service will provide you with four never before published romance titles every month! In fact, your books will be mailed to you at the same time advance copies are sent to book reviewers. You'll preview each of these new and unabridged books before they are released to the general public.

These books are filled with the kind of stories you have been longing for—stories of courtship, chivalry, honor, and virtue. Strong characters and riveting plot lines will make you want to read on and on. Romance is not dead, and each of these romantic tales will remind you that Christian faith is still the vital ingredient in an intimate relationship filled with true love and honest devotion.

Sign up today to receive your first set. Send no money now. We'll bill you only $9.97 post-paid with your shipment. Then every month you'll automatically receive the latest four "hot off the press" titles for the same low post-paid price of $9.97. That's a savings of 50% off the $4.95 cover price. When you consider the exaggerated shipping charges of other book clubs, your savings are even greater!

THERE IS NO RISK—you may cancel at any time without obligation. And if you aren't completely satisfied with any selection, return it for an immediate refund.

TO JOIN, just complete the coupon below, mail it today, and get ready for hours of wholesome entertainment.

Now you can curl up, relax, and enjoy some great reading full of the warmhearted spirit of romance.